If the Fairy Tale Fits...

she'll live happily ever after!

In these contemporary twists on classic fairy tales from Harlequin Romance, allow yourself to be swept away on a jet-set adventure where the modern-day heroine is the star of the story. The journey toward happy-ever-after may not be easy, but in a land far away, true love will *always* result in their dreams coming true—especially with a little help from Prince Charming!

Get lost in the magic of...

Beauty and the Playboy Prince
by Justine Lewis

Part of His Royal World
by Nina Singh

Cinderella's Billion-Dollar Invitation
by Michele Renae

Beauty and the Brooding CEO
by Juliette Hyland

His Strictly Off-Limits Ballerina
by Kate Hardy

All available now!

Dear Reader,

When my editor asked me to do a romance inspired by a fairy tale, I loved the idea—especially because I'd been to see the ballet of Sleeping Beauty the previous evening! I wanted to have a slightly different take, so I gender-swapped it: we have Pippa (Prince Phillip) rescuing Rory (Aurora). But how could I get Rory to prick his finger and sleep for a hundred years in a modern world? That's when the medical romance author in me had a bright idea...

I was thrilled to bits to get to write a ballet book. I've always loved the music, but never had ballet lessons as a (very clumsy) child. After I went to see *Swan Lake* at my local theater, about five years ago, they emailed me asking if I'd like to try their adult beginner classes. I took the plunge, and they've been an absolute joy—Friday mornings are the highlight of my week.

Both Pippa (as a ballerina) and Rory (as an arts TV presenter) adore ballet...and ballet is what brings them together and makes them fall in love.

I hope you enjoy Pippa and Rory's journey.

With love,

Kate Hardy

HIS STRICTLY OFF-LIMITS BALLERINA

KATE HARDY

H Harlequin

ROMANCE

Harlequin®
ROMANCE

ISBN-13: 978-1-335-21634-2

His Strictly Off-Limits Ballerina

Recycling programs for this product may not exist in your area.

Harlequin Enterprises ULC
22 Adelaide St. West, 41st Floor
Toronto, Ontario M5H 4E3, Canada
www.Harlequin.com

Printed in U.S.A.

Kate Hardy has always loved books and could read before she went to school. She discovered Harlequin books when she was twelve and decided that this was what she wanted to do. When she isn't writing, Kate enjoys reading, cinema, ballroom dancing and the gym. You can contact her via her website, katehardy.com.

Books by Kate Hardy

Harlequin Romance

Crowning His Secret Princess
Tempted by Her Fake Fiancé
Wedding Deal with Her Rival
A Fake Bride's Guide to Forever

Harlequin Medical Romance

Twin Docs' Perfect Match

Second Chance with Her Guarded GP
Baby Miracle for the ER Doc

Yorkshire Village Vets

Sparks Fly with the Single Dad

Saving Christmas for the ER Doc
An English Vet in Paris
Pediatrician's Unexpected Second Chance

Visit the Author Profile page
at Harlequin.com for more titles.

For my Friday ballet classmates and teachers—
thank you for the joy you bring to my week

CHAPTER ONE

HE WAS THE most beautiful man Pippa had ever seen. Tall, with dark hair that flopped endearingly over his forehead and eyes the colour of cornflowers, he reminded her of an actor she'd had a huge crush on when she was a teenager. Despite the fact that it was the middle of the afternoon, he was wearing formal evening dress: a dinner jacket with a shawl lapel, a bow tie that matched his eyes as well as the silk handkerchief in his pocket, and a wing-tip shirt. She couldn't see his shoes, but she'd just bet they were handmade and highly polished.

She hadn't seen him around at the Fitzroy Theatre—she would *definitely* have noticed him—but clearly he was involved with organising today's fundraiser rather than just having a ticket to the garden party, because he was carrying what looked like a cashbox and a book of cloakroom tickets.

Prince Charming, come to help save the ballet company?

Or, rather, their roof. The Fitzroy Theatre was a Georgian building, literally creaking at the rafters. And work on listed buildings took for ever—arguing what work needed to be done, and how, was only the first stage. Finally Nathalie, the head of the Fitzroy Ballet Company, had lost her temper and pointed out that the longer it was dragged out, the worse the damage would become, and she wasn't taking risks with a single member of her team or their audience. Not to mention how much longer it would take to fix—and how much more expensive it would be. And if enough work wasn't done over the summer and they were forced to cancel performances, was the surveyor planning to reimburse them for lost takings? Or was *monsieur* going to use his common sense? She wanted his report in her email by the end of the day, or *heads would roll*—just as they had in the Place de la Concorde. She'd finished with a tirade of French invective, using her hand to illustrate a guillotine blade.

Despite towering over the diminutive Frenchwoman, the surveyor had stammered an apology—and emailed his initial report to her as instructed. Nathalie had immediately swung into action, contacting their season ticket holders to ask for their help raising money for the repairs.

One of their patrons had offered something even better than money: the use of their garden for a party to raise funds. The ballet company had pooled all their contacts to get prizes for the raffle: everything from spa treatments to afternoon teas, tickets to shows and cases of wine, signed books and backstage passes.

The garden was absolutely stunning. Wisteria draped lushly over the back of the eighteenth-century rectory, filling the air with a heady scent. The herbaceous borders bloomed with flowers in soft shades of cream, lilac, pink and blue, and the wall at the back of the garden held espaliered apple trees that were still studded with blossoms. It was the sort of garden you could laze in and dream in, with a wildflower patch in one corner and a rectangle of soft, lush grass that made Pippa want to pirouette across it towards Prince Charming. Particularly as a string quartet and pianist from the Fitzroy's orchestra were currently playing the 'Dance of the Sugar Plum Fairy' in the drawing room that opened out onto the terrace.

Pippa had been the understudy for the Sugar Plum Fairy last year and knew the routine by heart. Though, much as she was tempted, she'd never take the risk of dancing on an unknown surface. A trip on a small, hidden bump could cause the kind of damage to her foot that would take her out of action for weeks. So she'd be sensible and stick to the role she and the rest of the dancers were playing this afternoon, alternating between meet-and-greets and carrying round silver platters of canapés. The bite-sized scone halves topped with strawberry conserve and clotted cream on her own tray looked absolutely delicious, and she fully intended to eat one after she'd handed them over to a colleague.

Tickets to the garden party had sold out rapidly. And hopefully people were buying extra glasses of champagne and lots of tickets for the raffle, from the gorgeous guy with the blue eyes—who'd just caught her eye and smiled at her, raising goosebumps on her skin. She smiled back, and he started walking towards her. All of a sudden it felt as if there wasn't enough air for her to breathe. Which was crazy, because they were outside and the air was limitless.

Nothing could beat an English walled garden on a sunny Sunday afternoon in May, Rory thought. The flowers were at peak prettiness; everyone seemed to be chatting and laughing and enjoying the ballet music played by a string quartet, which he presumed was part of the ballet company's orchestra.

His role this afternoon was to charm people into buying tickets for the raffle. He didn't mind giving up a Sunday to help, knowing how much his godmother adored ballet and that raising funds to help fix the Fitzroy's roof was important to her. Though he had to admit that he wasn't being *entirely* altruistic. The arts-based magazine show he hosted on a small commercial television channel had quietly gained a decent following, and he'd just pitched an idea for a series to his boss. He was pretty sure she'd agree to it; today would give him the opportunity to chat to the head of the Fitzroy Ballet Company and float the suggestion that one of their senior ballet dancers could appear in the series. In return, the publicity would help with the campaign for their roof, so it'd be a win for everyone.

He smiled, extolled the amazing prizes on the raffle table, talked to people, sold tickets and happily accepted donations. All was absolutely fine until he caught the eye of one of the waitresses. He'd noticed her earlier that afternoon and felt a jolt of recognition. Which was ridiculous, because he knew they'd never met. He would definitely have remembered her. But something about her drew him in, and it wasn't just that she was seriously pretty. There was something about her. She had *presence*.

Walking that gracefully with her tray, she had to be one of the dancers rather than one of the backstage team. She'd be perfect for his documentary. And snaffling one of the bite-sized scones would be a great excuse to talk to her.

When he caught her eye, he smiled at her. She smiled back. And it felt like more than just a polite gesture to a stranger; it felt like the beginning of something. Something unexpected. Something irresistible. He couldn't help making his way across the garden to her.

But then, when he was standing next to her and looking into eyes the colour of a stormy sky, all words went out of his head.

This was crazy. He made a living from talking, for pity's sake. He was *good* with words. He was known for putting people at ease. Why was he suddenly so inarticulate and clumsy with her?

'I…um… Are you enjoying the party?' he asked.

Oh, way to go, Rory.

She was obviously working, not a guest.

But she smiled again, and it felt as if the whole garden had lit up. Dazzling. Which was crazy, because they were outside in a sunny garden, not in a dim room where someone had just switched on a light.

'Yes, I am.' She proffered the tray. 'Hello. I'm Pippa. Can I tempt you?'

Yes. She definitely could tempt him. Which

really unsettled Rory, because he'd sworn off relationships a year ago, when he'd realised that his latest girlfriend was yet another in the line of partners who didn't see him for himself. He was tired of discovering his girlfriends only wanted to date him because they thought he was on his way to being really famous and would take them with him, or because he was the younger son of the Earl of Riverford and they'd get into the society pages. So he'd taken himself off the market, to avoid the disappointment and hurt of realising that yet again he was invisible, and the surface glitter that he thought was unimportant was the thing that mattered most to his dates.

'Thank you,' he said, and took one of the mini scones.

He was about to take a bite when a shockingly unexpected white-hot pain lanced into his neck.

'Ow!' he said, putting his hand up to the sore spot. What the hell had that been?

Except now he was feeling a bit dizzy. Strange. And he didn't understand why. He hadn't had so much as a sip of champagne because he'd been busy circulating.

Her expression changed to concern. 'Are you all right?'

'No, I don't think I am,' he said, but his words

sounded as if he was talking through a mouthful of sand, and he wasn't altogether sure she'd understood him. He shook his head. At least, he hoped he had, because everything was closing in on him. 'Need h…' He tried swallowing, to clear his throat, but he couldn't—and it was hard to breathe. Even though the sun was warm, he felt cold and clammy. He took a step, staggered—and then everything went black.

Something was very badly wrong. His sudden pallor, slurring his words, and then the way he'd staggered before falling to the ground in a dead faint…

The last time Pippa had seen something like this was ten years ago at a dance rehearsal, when her best friend had accidentally eaten something containing almonds and had an anaphylactic reaction. Thankfully Pippa had known where Sasha kept her adrenaline kit and how to administer it, so her friend had been just fine; and Pippa had gone on a first-aid training course that she'd kept up to date ever since.

If, as she suspected, this was an anaphylactic reaction, time was of the essence.

Ambulance, first. She set the tray on the floor, fished her phone from her pocket, unlocked it and handed it to the woman next to her. 'Can you call 999 for me, please?' she asked. 'Tell them it's an anaphylactic reaction and we don't have adrenaline. We need them here *now*.'

'Got it,' the woman said, and tapped the number into the phone.

Next, Pippa knelt beside the prostrate man and patted his pockets. No sign of an adrenaline kit. Time for Plan B. She scooped the mini scones off the tray, then stood up again and banged it with her fist like a gong. The string quartet stopped playing, and there was a hush.

'If there's a doctor here, or anyone with allergies who has an adrenaline pen with them, please can you come over here right now?' she called loudly.

There was a murmur and some movement among the crowd, but no offers of adrenaline were forthcoming. No doctor, either.

Then, to Pippa's relief, one person came over to help: a middle-aged woman in a beautiful dress. 'I'm not a doctor, and I'm afraid I haven't kept my first aid training up since I retired from teaching five years ago,' she said, 'but anything's better than nothing. I'm Carolyn.'

'Pippa,' Pippa said.

'What do you need me to do?'

'We need to check him over, and we might need to do CPR,' she said, turning the unconscious man onto his back. Hopefully he hadn't hit his head in the wrong place when he'd fallen. It was really worrying that he still hadn't woken up.

'Hello,' she said loudly, tapping his shoulder in an attempt to wake him. 'Can you hear me?'

When he didn't respond, she undid his bow tie and loosened the collar of his shirt. There was a large red patch on his neck. She remembered him saying, *'Ow!'* Had he been stung? Was he allergic to venom?

She checked his airway was clear, then she and Carolyn began to do CPR, swapping every couple of cycles to give their arms a break.

'Oh, my God—Rory!' said Rosemary, the woman who owned the house, rushing over as Pippa and Carolyn swapped again. 'What happened?'

'He collapsed out of nowhere, but there's a red mark on his neck. Do you know if he's allergic to bees or wasps?' Pippa asked, continuing to do the compressions to Carolyn's count.

'I've no idea. There aren't any allergies on his mother's side—I'm his godmother,' Rosemary said. 'He offered to help here today.'

'The ambulance is on its way,' Pippa reassured her. 'I...um—he was selling tickets.' She gestured to the cashbox and tickets he'd dropped.

Rosemary scooped them up. 'Thank you. I'll

give them to one of the team, then go and wait outside for the ambulance.'

Pippa wasn't sure how often she and Carolyn swapped as they kept the chest compressions going, because time seemed to simply stop until finally the ambulance crew arrived. She was relieved to see one of the paramedics was carrying a defibrillator, and she kept going with the chest compressions while she filled them in on what had happened.

'It was a good call on your part,' the first paramedic said. 'And good work with the CPR. We'll take over now. Can you make sure everyone gives us some space?'

'Of course,' Pippa said; between them, she, Carolyn and Rosemary shepherded everyone out of the area, promising to update them as soon as there was news.

It took two attempts with the defibrillator, but at last Rory's heart was beating again. One of them administered the injection of adrenaline into Rory's thigh; then they lifted him onto the stretcher and put an oxygen mask over his face.

Rory still wasn't conscious, but at least he was breathing. And he was in the right hands, now, too, Pippa thought.

'Did you want to come in with him?' the paramedic asked.

'Me? We only met a few seconds before he

collapsed,' Pippa said. 'He probably won't even remember me. Maybe his godmother?' She squeezed Rosemary's hand in reassurance. 'I'll make sure everything's sorted here, and someone from the Fitzroy will stay until you get back.'

'Thank you, my dear,' Rosemary said. 'For everything you've done.'

'Anyone here would've done the same,' Pippa said.

CHAPTER TWO

AFTER THE PARAMEDICS had taken Rory and Rosemary to hospital, people started coming over to Pippa, praising her quick actions.

She smiled and moved the conversation on. 'I only just met Rory, but this place belongs to his godmother, so I'm sure he'd want everyone to carry on enjoying the garden party. And, as he was selling raffle tickets, I'm sure he'd want people to keep buying them or donate to the roof fund.'

She cleared up the scones she'd scooped off the metal tray, then washed her hands, refilled her tray in the kitchen, and went to do the next bit of meet-and-greet.

Rosemary came back two hours later, when the garden party was winding down and people were helping to clear away tables and chairs. 'You saved Rory's life,' she said to Pippa. 'His parents are at the hospital with him now, and he's awake and talking again. He asked me to pass on his thanks, and ask whether you would mind giving me your details so he can say thank you himself?'

'It wasn't just me. Carolyn did the CPR with me—though I think she already left,' Pippa said. 'I'm sorry—I didn't think to take her details.'

'I'm so grateful to you both,' Rosemary said. 'I'm very fond of my godson.' Her face was still drawn with worry. 'The thought of how nearly we lost him…'

'He's in the right place,' Pippa said gently. 'The hospital will look after him. Let me know if there's anything else I can do.'

'Thank you.' Rosemary took down Pippa's number and gave her a hug.

The next morning, Rory lay in the hospital bed, still feeling a bit groggy and very much out of sorts. According to the medics, it was possible to have a second severe allergic reaction, almost like an aftershock, so it made sense for him to stay in the hospital for a bit longer. But he would rather be somewhere much quieter and more relaxed, and not hooked up to monitors that beeped all the time.

He'd seen the panic in his mother's eyes when she'd arrived at his bedside, and the fear that she'd lose him. The love mixed with the worry.

And he'd felt horribly guilty for scaring her, even though it hadn't been intentional.

Coming to terms with your own mortality wasn't easy, either. The doctor had told him that he'd need to carry around two auto-injectors of adrenaline all the time, in case he was ever stung again. Not only was he likely to react badly the next time he was stung by a wasp, the odds were that his reaction would be even more severe.

How could a creature so tiny—a centimetre and a half long, less than a hundredth of his height—have the power to kill him?

He could have *died*.

If it hadn't been for the quick thinking of the woman he'd been talking to, he wouldn't be here now. He owed her everything.

Rosemary, his godmother, had promised to find out his rescuer's name and get her details so he could thank her personally. At the very least, she deserved an armful of flowers.

Flowers that, ironically, he would need to avoid, in future, in case there was a hidden wasp. Ditto walking barefoot on a lawn, along with other delights he'd taken for granted in the summer. Enjoying a cool drink was out of the question, in case a wasp crawled into the can or bottle of beer he was drinking. Picnics were an equally bad idea, in case a wasp was attracted by the sweet scent of fruit. And no flapping the wasps away, because a panicking wasp emitted alarm pheromones which would summon other members of the colony to come to their rescue.

Just one teeny, tiny sting could pack one hell of a punch. In his case, not just the brief sharp, burning pain, or the minor swelling that normal people experienced for a few hours. His reaction had been systemic, affecting his breathing and stopping his heart.

Even now, the morning after, despite the prompt medical treatment he'd received, Rory still didn't feel great. Though he had to admit part of that feeling was mental rather than physical. His parents were insisting on picking him up from hospital tomorrow afternoon and taking him back to their London townhouse for a few days' rest. He loved his parents dearly, but he knew they'd spend the whole time wrapping him in cotton wool—and he wanted his life to go back to normal. Right back to how it had been Before Wasp. The life he'd planned and really, really loved.

Trying to distract himself, he flicked onto the internet on his phone and looked up the Fitzroy Ballet Company. His rescuer had walked like a dancer, so the chances were high that he'd find her somewhere on their website.

And there she was, listed under First Soloists. Pippa Barnes.

He clicked on the thumbnail of her face, and was rewarded with another picture, this time with her dressed as the Sugar Plum Fairy and executing a perfect pirouette. Her biography wasn't quite what he'd expected, though. Like him, she was the youngest of three. Her parents were both doctors, as were her two sisters; maybe that explained how she'd known what to do when he'd collapsed.

But Pippa hadn't gone to ballet school from the age of eleven, as the preliminary research for his series had led him to expect a high-level ballerina would've done. She'd taken ballet classes and exams, but she'd gone to a normal school and done her GCSEs and A levels. Then, at the age of eighteen, she'd swapped medical school for a place at a well-known ballet school, before joining the Fitzroy Ballet Company as an artist. Her rise through the ranks had been rapid: promoted to First Artist at the age of twenty-one, Soloist at twenty-two and First Soloist at twenty-three.

Rory read various articles and discovered that Pippa was widely tipped to be promoted to Principal Dancer this year—when she turned twenty-five. She was a real rising star in the world of ballet. She'd be perfect for his TV show. And maybe including her in the series would help her career, too; if she didn't make Principal Dancer with the Fitzroy this year, another company might spot the opportunity and snap her up.

He managed to shower and dress, which made him feel a bit more human, and was sitting normally in a chair, making notes, when his mother arrived.

'What are you doing?' Helena asked, frowning. 'You're supposed to be resting and letting yourself get better.'

'Sitting still and doing nothing is my idea of a nightmare,' Rory said.

Plus he'd spent too much time brooding already. At least when he was working he was too busy to ponder on his personal life—on the loneliness that had started to creep in, during quiet moments. But being alone was better than wasting his time with yet another girlfriend who only wanted him for what he could give her. He already had a family who loved him. He didn't need to find Ms Right and follow in his brother's and sister's footsteps. He was doing just fine on his own; and work helped him ignore any of the niggles about his love life.

'Besides, I have a series to plan. My boss gave me the green light for my documentary, this morning.'

Her eyes widened. 'Surely you're not intending to go back to work so soon?'

'Mum, I'm fine,' he reassured her. 'Luckily I've got a few pieces in hand, but I still need to do the live interview segment on Friday. I don't want to let anyone down.'

'Rory, you nearly *died* yesterday.'

Helena Fanshawe, the Countess of Riverford, was famous for being unflappable. When the King was still the Prince of Wales, she'd hosted him for afternoon tea with next to no notice. The fact that his mother was making a fuss now was a huge red flag for Rory.

'Mum, I know, but I've worked hard to get where I am now and I don't want to slip back,' he said, as gently as he could. 'I'm planning to spend a couple of minutes on the show warning people about wasp allergies. I was incredibly lucky because Pippa Barnes knew what to do and she saved my life. I want to pay that forward and give my audience the same knowledge.'

'That's a fair point,' Helena agreed. 'Though you do need to rest. Remember, they had to restart your heart.'

'Mmm.' Thankfully he didn't remember anything other than his throat feeling full of sand and then passing out, but he still had a sore patch of skin on his chest from the defibrillator pad. The nurse had suggested using aloe vera gel to cool the burn. Maybe he could distract his mother with that; or maybe such a visible reminder would worry her even more. He decided to keep it to himself.

'Why don't you let yourself get over it this week,' Helena continued, 'and go back to doing the show next week? Let someone else step in, just this once?'

'No. I won't take any stupid risks, Mum,' Rory promised. 'But I don't want to live the rest of my life holding myself back because I'm scared of encountering another wasp.'

She didn't say a word, but the worry was all there in her eyes.

What if he was *stung by another wasp? Would he die, next time?*

That was a question he didn't want to think about.

'Mum, please stop worrying. I'll carry the two adrenaline pens with me all the time, and I've got a diary note of their expiry date on my phone so I can make sure I always have medication with me that's in date. I have a card in my wallet right in front of my driving licence, telling people that I'm severely allergic to wasp stings and how to use the adrenaline.' He stood up and gave her a hug. 'Remember, I learned how to deal with any situation from the amazingly capable and calm woman who brought me up. And, before you say it, that's not flattery. It's a fact.'

Helena rested her forehead against his shoulder. 'I want you to keep your independence, Rory. Of course I do. And I know you're sensible. But we came so close to losing you yesterday. I've never felt fear like that before. Or such helplessness,' she admitted. 'I'm your mother, and I'm supposed to be able to protect you from everything. Yesterday, I couldn't, and I'm finding that hard to handle.' Her voice cracked. 'So forgive me if I wrap you in cotton wool a little too much, because right now I'm terrified that you might...' A single tear brimmed over her lashes, and she brushed it away. 'Sorry.'

'Oh, Mum.' His own voice was croaky, now. 'It isn't your fault, or Dad's. An allergy to wasps isn't hereditary. It can happen out of nowhere, even if you've been stung before and not reacted.'

'Rory...' She shook her head. 'I'm trying very hard not to fuss over you. But I really want you to stay with us for the rest of the week. Just so...'

'...you know I'm safe,' he finished. 'I get that, and I don't want you to worry. Let's compromise. I'll stay with you, but I'll be in the studio as usual on Friday.'

She gave him her best mum glare, clearly trying to make him back down and take the rest of the week off.

He stared back just as stubbornly, because he was absolutely going to do the job he loved. The job he *needed*. Without his job, who was he?

She sighed. 'All right. We'll compromise. But I'll drive you to the studio and your father will pick you up afterwards.'

He'd made his point. Time to give a little. 'You can stay in the audience, if you promise not to heckle.'

She gave him a rueful smile. 'All right. And, while we're waiting for the doctor to see if he'll discharge you tomorrow, you can tell me all about this new series.'

Around lunchtime on Wednesday—when he hoped that Pippa wouldn't be busy in rehearsals—Rory called her mobile. As it started to ring, the butterflies in his stomach seemed to do a stampede.

This was utterly ridiculous.

He interviewed famous people for a living. People who'd won big awards, actors and musicians who were household names and had been at the top of their field for decades. Talking to a rising star in the ballet world shouldn't make

him feel this nervous. Plus he'd already practised what to say.

But the first time he'd actually spoken to
Pippa—the only time, he amended wryly—all
the words had gone out of his head. And then
he'd collapsed.

No wasps. There were no wasps. It wasn't
going to happen this time, he reminded himself.

The line stopped ringing. 'Hello?'

'Pippa? It's Rory Fanshawe. You kindly gave
my godmother your number.' Oh, and now he
was gabbling like a teenager. He forced himself to slow down. 'I wanted to thank you for
saving my life.'

'You're very welcome.'

She had a really nice voice, he thought. Kind.
Sweet. Calm. 'I wondered if I could take you to
lunch or something? To say thank you in person,
I mean,' he added hastily. He didn't want her to
think he was trying to hit on her. Because he
wasn't. This was a combination of good manners and work.

'That's lovely of you to offer, but there's
no need. Besides, I wasn't the only one who
helped,' she pointed out. 'Carolyn did the CPR
with me.'

Pippa wasn't taking the sole credit for saving
his life; he liked that even more. And he was
pleased that he was one step ahead on that front.

'I've already managed to get hold of Carolyn,' he said. 'I'm taking her to lunch next week.'

'Oh.' Pippa sounded surprised.

'It's the least I can do.' He paused. 'Are you free for lunch any time this week? Or next week?' he added, considering that it was already Wednesday.

'I only get a half an hour break between my class and rehearsal,' she warned.

'You still take classes?' He hadn't expected that.

'Every dancer takes classes, even the Principal Dancers. Whatever the stage of your career, you never stop learning,' she said.

The more he listened to Pippa talk, the more Rory was sure that she'd be perfect for his show. She was clear, articulate and could tell people who were interested in a career in dance exactly what to expect. He ignored the little voice in his head saying that the real reason he wanted to see her was because he'd felt more attracted to her at the garden party than he had been to anyone in months. This was an opportunity to get the perfect expert for his documentary. And that would keep the flare of attraction nicely damped down, because working with her would make her off-limits. He wasn't risking his series for a couple of dates that would no doubt turn out to be as disappointing as his last few.

Even though she didn't seem like the last few women he'd dated, he'd been burned once too often to want to take a chance. 'Would you be free tomorrow?' he asked.

'Yes.'

'I assume your class is held somewhere near the Fitzroy?'

'All our classes are held at the Fitzroy,' she said.

'Tell me what time to meet you,' he said, 'and either let me know the name of a place you like nearby so I can book a table—and we can preorder lunch so we don't have to spend all your time waiting for food—or I can bring us an indoor picnic.' That way, they could avoid wasps. 'Do you have any allergies or dietary requirements?'

'No allergies and I eat almost anything,' she said. 'Your picnic idea sounds really good. The theatre restaurant isn't open at lunchtime, so we can use one of the tables there. Classes end at half-past twelve.'

'Wonderful. Thank you,' he said. 'I'll see you tomorrow at half-past twelve.' He'd been to the ballet before with his godmother, so he remembered the layout of the theatre. 'In the foyer next to the box office?'

'That'd be perfect,' she said.

Rory was smiling as he ended the call. Next,

he'd call Nathalie Charrier, the founder of the Fitzroy Ballet Company, and run his ideas past her—just as he'd originally planned to do at the garden party, before a wasp had turned his life into chaos.

And, even though he told himself that the thrill he felt was simply the buzz he always had when he was working on a new idea, part of him had to admit the truth: he was really looking forward to seeing Pippa Barnes again tomorrow. And it wasn't strictly work.

CHAPTER THREE

PIPPA WAS DEFINITELY guilty of using muscle memory to get through the warm-up in class on Thursday morning rather than listening to the teacher. Demi-pliés, slow tendus, port de bras...

Because her head was full of Rory Fanshawe, and the fact that she was having lunch with him today.

She shook herself, knowing how ridiculous she was being. It wasn't anything like a date. He'd told her that he wanted to thank her in person for saving his life, and he was having lunch with Carolyn next week for exactly the same reason. It was more than likely that he was already involved with someone else. And, even if he *was* single, she didn't have time for any kind of relationship. Not if she wanted to make Principal Dancer this year. And she really, really wanted that promotion. Getting to the top position would prove once and for all that she was good enough. That all the hard work and sacrifice had been worth it. That she'd made the right decision when she'd chosen ballet over a career in medicine, disappointing her family.

'Pippa, did you hear what I said?'

Jeanne, their artistic director, sounded sharp. Given that Jeanne was one of the people Pippa needed to impress, letting herself daydream in class was a very stupid thing to do.

'I'm so sorry,' Pippa said. 'Would you mind repeating that?'

Jeanne rapped out instructions, and Pippa forced her mind off Rory and on to what she was supposed to be doing. She was careful to give the class her full attention after that, but even so Jeanne had a quiet word with her at the end.

'My advice is, keep your focus,' Jeanne said, her eyes glinting a warning. 'I'd hate to see you waste your opportunities.'

Wasting her chances because she was dreaming of someone unsuitable. Not that Jeanne had any idea who she was dreaming about, but losing her focus was unprofessional. Unacceptable.

Pippa felt the heat flood through her cheeks. 'I'm sorry. It won't happen again.'

'Good.' Jeanne strode off.

Pippa changed swiftly. She didn't have time to worry about whether her T-shirt and leggings were suitable; besides, this was an indoor picnic, so it really didn't matter what she wore, did it? As a concession to being outside work hours, she released her dark hair from the tight bun she wore for classes and rehearsals, and hurried out into the foyer.

Rory was standing next to the box office, as they'd arranged. He was carrying a woven willow picnic basket in one hand and a stunning bouquet in the other: stocks, roses, chrysanthemum and freesia, all in shades of pink and pale cream.

'Thank you for saving my life, Pippa,' he said, handing her the flowers.

She buried her nose in them, inhaling the sweet scents. 'You're very welcome. I'm glad you're OK.' Though he still looked tired; no doubt he hadn't had much rest in hospital. 'And thank you very much for these. You really didn't have to, but they're absolutely gorgeous.'

'They have their own water so you don't need to find a vase for them until you can get them home,' he added. 'I have to admit, I did have the odd twinge of nerves between the florist's and here, in case a stray wasp spotted them and sideswiped me on the way. But fortunately there were no vespine encounters.'

His smile was incredibly cute. And it was a nice change to meet a man who admitted his vulnerabilities instead of putting on a performance. In his shoes, having almost died from a sting, she'd be terrified of doing anything that might attract a wasp. But he'd used an odd word. 'Vespine?' she queried.

'Waspy,' he said. 'From *vespa*, the Latin for wasp.'

Given that his accent was slightly on the posh side, she wasn't surprised he knew Latin. He'd probably studied it at school. She smiled back. 'Shall we go and sit down?'

She led the way to the restaurant space. Some of the other dancers were sitting in the area, scrolling on their phones as they ate; normally she would've joined them, but today she found a quiet table.

Rory undid the picnic basket, shook out a red-and-white-checked tablecloth, then deftly unpacked two enamel plates, bamboo cutlery, glasses, a bottle of spring water in what looked like an ice jacket, and an array of food in reusable tubs.

She blinked. 'Wow. I was expecting maybe a sandwich, some fruit and a coffee from the shop round the corner. This is amazing.' A real picnic. A *posh* picnic. The sort that people would take to Glyndebourne.

'I looked up the best nutrition for ballet dancers, and based it on that,' he said. 'You said you were working this afternoon; the website recommended lean protein, veggies and whole-grains. I hope you like something here.'

Cold poached salmon, slices of chicken breast, chunks of avocado, a salad of quinoa with edamame beans and tenderstem broccoli, cold roasted Mediterranean vegetables, baby plum tomatoes and watercress—all beautifully presented. Pippa wasn't sure whether he'd bought it all at a deli or whether he'd prepared some of it himself at home, but he'd obviously put a lot of thought into the menu and she appreciated the effort.

'There are strawberries, blueberries and Greek yogurt for pudding,' he added.

'This is perfect. Thank you so much,' she said. 'This is a real treat.'

'Please, help yourself,' he said. 'Water?'

'Thank you.' She filled her plate while he filled her glass. 'How are you feeling?'

'Fine.'

But it was said a little too breezily. And those beautiful blue eyes didn't meet her gaze. 'Really?' she asked.

He sighed. 'I'm a little bit twitchy because of what happened, but I need to get back to normal sooner rather than later. The longer I leave it, the bigger the gap will be between BW and AW.'

'Before wasp and after wasp?' she guessed.

He gave her a wry smile. 'Exactly. And it doesn't help that my mother's wrapping me in a ton of cotton wool. We had a deal—if I stay with her and Dad this week, she won't give me a hard time about working tomorrow night. I thought we'd muddle through OK, but she's driving me mad, constantly worrying about me and checking on me. I'm carrying adrenaline pens and an instruction card, and I'm not going to do anything to risk…' He wrinkled his nose. 'Well.'

'Vespine encounters,' she said.

'Exactly. I've been trying to convince her that I'm not going to walk barefoot in Rosemary's garden, especially near the fruit trees when the apples have fallen, or sit anywhere near a wastebin on a summer day. And I won't be drinking anything in a can that's *remotely* attractive to wasps.'

'But you did carry these gorgeous flowers here,' she pointed out. 'Wasps like flowers. Especially ones that smell as lovely as stocks.'

He groaned. 'The florist is a three-minute walk away from the theatre. And I can't live in a sterile bubble for the rest of my life, Pippa. It's about being practical. Minimising the risks and living my life as normally as I can.'

She could understand that. 'You said you were going to work tomorrow night. What do you do?' She'd meant to look him up on the internet, but she'd been so busy at work that she hadn't had time.

'I'm a broadcast journalist.'

Working with words would also explain why he was comfortable using terms like 'vespine'. 'Broadcast. Does that mean radio rather than newspapers or magazines?' she asked.

'TV,' he said, but his tone was matter-of-fact rather than boasting.

So was he famous? How embarrassing that she didn't know who he was. 'Sorry. I'm usually working in the evening, and I don't watch much TV,' she explained.

He smiled ruefully. 'I wasn't trying to show off or do the whole "dear girl, don't you know who I *am*?" thing,' he said, hamming up the quote in a way that made her laugh.

He didn't come across as an entitled celeb; he didn't have that hard, arrogant edge. She found him easy to talk to; he made her feel that he was listening to what she was saying.

'Though if you ever watch programmes about the arts in your free time, you *might* have heard of me,' he said.

'Sorry,' she said again.

'Don't apologise. You're busy making art rather than talking about it or watching it,' he said.

'So how did you become a broadcast journalist?' she asked.

'I did some work with university radio as a student, then started my own podcast,' he said.

'I got a job as a researcher in TV when I gradu-
ated, then had the chance to do some interviews
myself. Then I worked my way up to being the
lead on a show on an arts channel. It goes out
at nine p.m. on a Friday night, though it's not
live—we film the chat bit in the studio in the
afternoon.'

'Tell me about your show,' she invited, intrigued.

'The first half is a round-up—snippets from
new exhibitions or shows and brief interviews
with the people involved. Actually, I love that
bit of it,' he said, warming to his theme, 'because I get to talk to everyone from musicians
and artists to writers and curators and there's
always something new and fresh. The second
half is more of a chat show, with guests in the
studio.'

'Nine p.m. If it's a show night, I'm on stage; if
it's not a show night, I'm most probably asleep,'
she confessed.

He smiled. 'I'm not trying to impress you.
It's just what I do. I know I'm very privileged
because I can share people's joy in their jobs,
as well as my own love of the arts.'

'Loving what you do is important,' she said.
'And I'm lucky in that way, too.'

'I wasn't stalking you,' he said, 'but I wanted
to know a bit more about the person who saved

my life, so I read your bio on the Fitzroy website, and a couple of articles. Your path to ballet looks a little bit different to everyone else's.'

She felt herself tense, and hoped he hadn't noticed. She *was* different. It was part of the reason why she had to work so hard. 'My parents are doctors,' she said carefully. 'So are my sisters. I'm the baby of the family. Everyone thought I'd be a doctor, too.' More than thought it. *Expected* it.

'You had a place at medical school, but you swapped it for ballet,' he said. 'Why?'

Because it was her dream. She'd tried to make herself do what her parents wanted, but she hadn't been able to give up on that. 'I fell in love with dance, right from my first ballet class as a four-year-old,' she said simply. 'The music and the movements, how they fit together and the way it makes me feel…it's all I've ever wanted to do. Even though I knew it wouldn't be an easy career, with lots of people all chasing the same parts, that didn't put me off. I don't mind the long hours rehearsing and honing my craft outside performances, or the unsociable working hours.' All the downsides of the job that her parents had pointed out in great detail. She gave him her best professional smile, not wanting him to know how hard the choice had been: disappoint her family, or spend her life doing something she didn't love. Whichever way she decided, she'd lose something.

'Getting that first break—no matter how hard you work—always involves a bit of luck,' she continued. 'My parents wanted me to have proper academic qualifications to fall back on; they said dance school would limit my options too much. Eventually we compromised. I did the academic stuff they wanted, and they let me have private lessons to make up for what I was missing at ballet school. I applied to university, but we agreed if I was accepted to ballet school they'd give me three years after my training to make it work. If I couldn't, then I'd go to university and train as a doctor instead.' Hopefully she'd made it sound a lot less painful than it had been. Her parents hadn't shouted or screamed or slammed doors; but the quiet disappointment in their eyes every time they looked at her had pierced a lot, lot deeper. And it had hardened her resolve to let nothing distract her until she got to the very top of her profession.

'Three science A levels *and* intensive ballet classes? It sounds as if you had to do twice the work,' he said.

She had. It had really polished her time-management skills. 'It was worth it,' she said. 'Now, I get to do what I love every single day. When I eventually become Principal Dancer, I know I'll only have a few years at my peak before I'll need to switch to directing, choreography or teaching, but right now I'm really living the dream.' She smiled. 'And that's without the rose-tinted specs. You?'

'Massively privileged,' he said. 'I could've joined the family business, but I'm the spoiled baby and, unlike yours, my parents let me do what I loved. For me, it was words. And I had some lucky breaks.' He smiled at her. 'Actually, speaking of work, I wanted to run a couple of things by you.'

She frowned. 'What sort of things?'

'Are you working tomorrow night?' he asked.

'Yes. Why?'

'Because I'd like to do a piece about the hidden danger of the summer arts season,' he said. 'This is the time of year when people go to outdoor concerts and performances—the Proms, Glyndebourne, garden parties at stately homes. Did you know that nearly three in a hundred people have a severe reaction to wasp stings?'

'No.'

'Neither did I,' he said, 'until it happened to me. I want to do a piece to camera about it. From my point of view as someone felled by a wasp; from a doctor about what to do if someone collapses in front of you; and from yours about how it feels to rescue someone. Plus,' he added, as if to head off her immediate refusal, 'you can mention the Fitzroy fundraiser in passing, because that was what you were doing when you rescued me.'

'Me, on TV?'

'I think you'd be a natural. You have a good voice for broadcasting,' he said. 'As you're working tomorrow night, maybe I could film you during your lunchbreak?'

'I'd need to think about it,' she said. 'And to talk to Nathalie, our director. I need her permission before I do anything.'

'Actually, I spoke to Nathalie earlier,' he said. 'Because that was only one of my proposals. The other is that my boss has given me the green light to make a small series about dance.'

'Dance is a big subject,' she said.

'Which is why I get to do a series rather than a single show,' he said. 'I'm looking at the history of certain dance types, one per episode, talking a bit about famous dancers in history and the present, and there'll be a section where a professional dancer teaches me a routine over the course of a week.'

'What types of dance are you covering?' she asked.

'Ballet—which is where I'd like you to help— ballroom, tango, and disco.' He grinned. 'My mum says if I can get John Travolta to teach me disco and I let her be my runner so he dances just once with her, she'll be my PA for an entire year.'

Pippa chuckled. 'My mum loved *Grease*.'

'Mine watches the film when she's had a bad day.' He smiled back. 'It's like what you were saying earlier—my show's going to look at the work that goes into a performance and what happens behind the scenes. I want to show a dancer's journey from complete novice to reaching performance standard. A bit like *Strictly*, but without the knockout competition.'

'Isn't that the point of *Strictly*? The competition bit, I mean?' she asked.

'It's not the only point,' he said. 'My theory is that what the audience loves best is seeing the dancer's journey. Obviously the audience has their favourites, but have you noticed that they always root for the underdog? And they're always more excited about the dancers who don't have a clue to start with, rather than the ones who already have dance experience.'

She thought about it. 'That's true. But you said you want a professional to teach you a routine. Do you have any dance experience?'

'Not really,' he said. 'I learned to do the waltz when I was younger, but apart from that I've never done any formal dance training. If I went clubbing at uni I just did what everyone else did.' He looked at her. 'I was planning a video diary showing my progress, all the highs and lows. The audience will see me go from someone who's never even tried to do a pirouette to someone who's confident enough to dance a whole piece, and hopefully they'll see the moment when I'm close to giving up and then it clicks.' He paused. 'What do you think? Would you be up for being part of the show and teaching me a routine?'

Being on TV.

It would really boost her profile as a dancer.

'I'd need to clear it with Nathalie before I could even start to think about it,' she said.

'Actually, she gave me permission to ask you,' Rory said, 'but of course you'll want to talk it over with her before you make a decision. And I'm not going to pressure you for an answer within the next five minutes. We have plenty of time.'

'What kind of routine are you looking for? Something traditional, or something modern?' Pippa had always thought that choreography was a potential option for her in the future after she'd finished her performance career, but she hadn't taken it further than thinking about it. This was a chance to learn something new, open another door.

'I'm happy to hear suggestions,' he said.

'From *Strictly*, I know that the male contestants have a slightly harder job because they have to learn to lead.'

'It's not quite like that in ballet,' she said. 'In a pas de deux, the male dancer tends to support the female dancer and the attention's on her rather than on him. So a traditional pas de deux won't really work for your purposes. I could teach you a simplified version of a variation— a solo,' she clarified. 'Something where your audience would recognise the music. Maybe something a ballerina would normally do en pointe, but we can adapt the footwork to suit you. Not because you're male,' she added, 'but because you need years of strength and mobility training first. Otherwise you risk really damaging your feet and ankles. I could adapt something to demi-point—tiptoes,' she explained. She thought about it for a moment. 'Maybe the "Dying Swan". Actually, that'd be a good one because it'll show how a dancer tells a story.'

He shook his head. 'Not a solo. The other thing about *Strictly* is that the audience likes to see the celebrity and the professional dance together.'

Something sensual, like a rumba; or something romantic, like a waltz. *A choreographed love story...*

The idea sent an unexpected ripple through her, which she suppressed instantly.

Absolutely not.

Rory Fanshawe might look like a fairytale prince and have excellent manners, but Pippa wasn't looking to fall in love with anyone. She didn't have the time or the space for romance in her life. Getting distracted by a relationship would mean not giving her all to her job—and then she'd be less likely to get the promotion she was working so hard for. She'd come so far; she didn't want to lose her chances now.

Guilt twinged somewhere underneath her ribcage. She wouldn't be able to give enough time to a relationship, either. She knew she didn't give enough to her family as it was. She was rubbish at staying in touch with her sisters, rubbish at being a dutiful daughter—and she'd be just as inadequate as a girlfriend, with her unsociable working hours and the fact that all her energies went into dancing.

'If you want a duet, then maybe I can teach your partner to dance, too,' she suggested.

And then she wished she hadn't opened her mouth, because that sounded as if she was fishing.

Which she wasn't. Was she?

'No partner,' he said after a beat. And then he looked her straight in the eye. 'Would your partner have a problem with me taking up your time between rehearsals and classes?'

Well, she deserved that one. She'd asked him a personal question first. 'No partner,' she said, echoing his words. Though Rory had just given her the perfect out. She didn't have time to teach him. No way could she take an entire week off work to teach him and be filmed.

But, before she could refuse, another thought slid into her head. In a month's time, the company would start their summer break. It would be the perfect time for her to work on Rory's project. And hadn't he said that they had plenty of time?

'I'll talk to Nathalie,' she said. Then her phone started playing three long rings—the sound to signal the end of an interval in the theatre, which she'd used as the ringtone for her alarm. 'That's lunch over,' she said regretfully. 'Sorry. I need to get back.'

'No problem. You did tell me you only had half an hour. I appreciate you giving up the time.'

She smiled. 'Thank you for lunch and the flowers.'

'My pleasure. I'm not pressuring you for an answer about the series,' he said, 'but if you could let me know later today about the two minutes or so to camera I'd need from you tomorrow about your experience saving a life when you were supposed to be saving a roof, that'd be great.'

'All right,' she said. 'I'll message you.'

Rory watched Pippa walk gracefully out of the restaurant area before he packed up the remains of their picnic. He really hoped she'd agree to do the show; she was articulate, passionate about her subject, dedicated to her career, and he thought he could learn a lot from her.

And she was single…

He pushed the thought away. The last couple of years, his social life had been a complete mess, with the women he'd dated interested in either Rory the up-and-coming TV presenter, or Rory the youngest son of the Earl of Riverford. None of them had seemed interested in who he was behind that, and he'd felt so let down. Was it so much to ask, to be seen for who he really was instead of his public persona? And every time he realised someone was only with him because of what he could give her, it had disappointed him more. It had made him miserable, to the point where it was easier just to focus on his job and enjoy spending his free time with his family instead.

Though the wasp incident had stirred up a few other things in his head, when he'd been stuck in hospital with too much time to think. What did he really want from life? Did he want to become a national treasure, with his own chat show on prime-time Saturday night TV? Did he want to take the more serious route and produce documentaries? Should he go back to the family business he'd sidestepped discussing with Pippa? Or did he want to settle down, the way his brother and sister had, and start a family of his own?

Though making decisions when he was feeling so out of sorts would only lead to making the wrong one. Maybe he just needed a little time for things to settle again. Time to have fun. To remind himself how good it felt to be alive—without letting himself give in to the fear that it could all vanish in a second.

CHAPTER FOUR

AT THE END of rehearsal, Pippa headed for Nathalie's office and rapped on the door.

'Come in!'

Pippa ignored her boss's slightly fierce tone, guessing that Nathalie had been dealing with builders, and walked in with a smile. 'Do you have a couple of minutes, please, Nathalie?'

'As it's you, yes. What's it about?'

Typical Nathalie, not bothering with small talk. 'I wanted some advice,' Pippa said.

'Would that have anything to do with Rory Fanshawe?'

Pippa nodded. 'He said he'd already run things past you and you'd given him the go-ahead to talk to me. And I wanted to double-check you'd be happy for him to interview me about what happened at the garden party. He wants to do that tomorrow so it can go on his show tomorrow night.'

Nathalie nodded. 'It's a good opportunity to raise your profile. The figures on his show are very respectable. He suggested interviewing you in front of the Fitzroy, and he'll mention our roof.'

'I feel a bit of a fraud, though. Plenty of people know how to do CPR,' Pippa said.

'And plenty don't,' Nathalie reminded her. 'Or know what an anaphylactic reaction looks like. He was very lucky you were there.'

'OK. I'll tell him I'll do it.'

'Good.' Nathalie rested her elbows on her desk and steepled her fingers. 'Did he mention his other project to you?'

Pippa nodded. 'It sounds fun. But I can hardly ask you for a week off to do it.'

'Of course you can ask, *chérie*,' Nathalie said silkily. 'But the answer would be no.' She paused. 'Just as it would be for Yuki.'

Yuki Ito was the other candidate for promotion to Principal Dancer; although they were friends, rather than deadly rivals, they were both very aware that there was only one slot. Pippa liked the other ballerina and rated her talent, but she really wanted to be the one who got the top job. It would validate the choice she'd made. And maybe then she'd finally stop feeling that she'd let her family down by not following in their footsteps.

As Nathalie's words sank in, the situation became horribly clear. 'He's asking Yuki as well?'

'He's asking you first, because you saved his life. If you don't want to do it, then Yuki would be the obvious next choice,' Nathalie said.

Pippa shook herself. The promotion was something she couldn't influence. All she could do was work hard, dance to the best of her ability, and hope that the Fitzroy's management team thought she was good enough. But doing the show... She'd liked what Rory had told her; she knew she'd enjoy the challenge of choreographing a piece and teaching a complete novice how to do it well.

Would it be a distraction, working with Rory—the way she'd let thoughts of him distract her in class this morning? Or would it give her the edge and show the team that she was capable of being a good ambassador for the Fitzroy and was ready to be promoted?

'What do you think about it?' Pippa asked carefully.

'I think,' Nathalie said, 'it needs to be your decision.'

Which didn't help in the slightest. She didn't have a clue what was going on in her boss's head. A snap decision would be the wrong one. 'I think,' Pippa said, 'I'll sleep on it. Make a list of the pros and cons.' And right at that moment she wasn't sure which column Rory Fanshawe would fit in. Possibly both.

She thought about it all the way home. A nap and a shower didn't make her thoughts any clearer. In the end, she grabbed her phone. Her sisters were both working part-time and this was the sweet spot between them getting home and settling the children down for dinner. Plus talking to Rory had made her think more about her family. It would be good to connect with her sisters. She was horribly aware that all too often they were the ones calling her, and she put off returning the calls on the grounds that it was too late to ring them, or she had a rehearsal. And then that made her feel she'd let them down, and it was easier just to bottle out of it and send a quick text instead of hearing the disappointment in their voices.

'Pips? Is everything all right?' Holly asked the second she answered the video call, looking concerned.

'Yes—are you all right?' Laura asked, joining them.

'Ye-es. I just wanted a bit of advice,' Pippa said.

'Now you're really worrying us. What's happened?' Holly asked.

'Nothing. Well, not *nothing*,' Pippa said. 'At the garden party fundraiser, one of the helpers was stung by a wasp. Anaphylaxis, nobody around with an adrenalin pen, so I had to do CPR. The paramedics had to shock him.'

'That's a tough situation,' Laura said. 'And well done, you. I assume he's OK?'

'Yes.' She paused. 'It turns out he has a TV show. He's doing a piece about wasps and what to do if someone reacts badly to a sting. And he's, um, interviewing me.'

'You're going to be on TV? That's fantastic! Which channel and when?' Holly asked.

'Tomorrow night, nine p.m.' She told them the channel.

'Hang on—that's Rory Fanshawe's show, isn't it?' Laura asked.

'You've seen his show?' Pippa was surprised; her oldest sister had never mentioned it before. Then again, she knew she hadn't really given Laura the chance to mention it. She kept most of their conversations light and easy, so she wouldn't have to face how she let her sisters down, too, by being so unavailable.

'I watch his show every week,' Laura said. 'I love the way he interviews people and gets the best out of them.'

'Me, too,' Holly said. 'Have you told Mum and Dad?'

'Not yet.' Pippa knew she ought to, but she also knew they'd focus on the fact that she was on TV because of medicine, not because of dance. And that would feel like another slap in the face.

'They won't want to miss seeing your first time on TV,' Laura said gently.

And now Pippa felt even guiltier. 'Sorry. Just… I know they wanted me to be a doctor. So did Gran and Gramps.'

'They all know how hard a career in the arts is,' Holly said. 'Mum and Dad just wanted you to have a safety net, in case it didn't work out. That's not the same as not believing in you, Pip.'

Pippa wasn't so sure. She'd really felt the pressure of her parents wanting her to make a different choice, and she still felt bad about not making the one that would've made them happy. 'Mmm.'

Laura came to her rescue. 'So what's the advice you wanted?'

'Rory's making a series about different dances—how they started, famous dancers, that sort of thing. And as part of it he needs a professional to teach him a routine. He asked me to do the ballet one,' Pippa explained.

'That's great! It'd look really good on your CV, too,' Holly said. 'Our little sister, the TV star.'

'It's only one programme,' Pippa reminded her.

'What does Nathalie think?' Holly asked.

'She says it's my decision.' Pippa grimaced. 'That's just it, Hol. If I do it, will I lose my focus? That could cost me the promotion. On the other hand, if I don't do it, will Nathalie think I don't have what it takes to make it to the very top?'

'You're the most focused person I've ever met,' Laura said. 'What makes you think doing the show will distract you?'

Pippa's face grew hot, and she hoped it wasn't as red as it felt.

But Holly was good at noticing things left unsaid. It was one of the reasons she was such a good doctor. 'You think Rory will distract you?' Holly asked. 'Mmm. He's very easy on the eye. I can see how he might…let's say, hold your attention.'

Pippa's face felt even hotter. 'I'm not in the market for a relationship.'

'We're not necessarily saying you need to date someone, but you do need a better work-life balance, Pip,' Laura said.

'More fun,' Holly added. 'Not just work, work and more work.'

'I love what I do. It's not like work,' Pippa protested.

'It's relentless, your schedule. I couldn't do it,' Laura said. 'You know you're always welcome here on your days off.'

'And mine. It's chaos, half the time, but it'll give you a break,' Holly suggested.

'I know. And I appreciate it,' Pippa said.

'But you're not going to take either of us up on the offer, because you want that promotion and you think working fifteen-hour days is the way to get it—which really *isn't* good for you, and I'm saying that both as your middle sister and with my GP hat on,' Holly said. 'I reckon you should do Rory's show. If Nathalie doesn't give you that promotion, then other ballet company directors will see the show and it could open some doors for you.'

'Agreed,' Laura said. 'Though I still think you need a proper break over the summer. Don't spend your entire break practising. Come to France with us. There's plenty of room in the villa.'

Her sisters, their husbands and children went away with her parents every summer for a fortnight, hiring a villa in Provence. They always invited Pippa, and she always turned them down because she was working or taking an extra class.

'All you have to do is sit in a garden, eating lovely French bread and cheese and strawberries, sip sparkling rosé, read a bit to the kids, and chill out with us,' Holly coaxed. 'We'll run interference if Mum or Dad try to talk you into keeping ballet as just a hobby. We get that ballet's your life.'

A life where she worked so hard to prove herself. 'We'll see,' Pippa said, not wanting to reject her sisters outright. She loved them, she really did. So why was it so hard to tell them that?

'If you won't come to France, then at least say yes to Rory,' Laura said.

'What if…?' Pippa stopped, not knowing how to frame the question.

'Do the coin test,' Holly said gently. 'Heads you do it, tails you don't. As soon as you see that head or tail on the back of your hand, you'll either be pleased or wish it had been the other one—and that will tell you what you *really* wanted to do.'

'I'll do that,' Pippa promised. 'Thank you both for listening.'

'That's what sisters are for,' Laura reassured her.

She lingered a bit longer, asking about her nieces and nephews and brothers-in-law, and she was thoughtful when she finally ended the call. Strange how they'd both assumed that something was wrong when she'd called. Did she really neglect her family so much?

Guilt throbbed through her. She was so focused on proving she'd made the right career decision that, yes, when she looked at it, she *did* neglect her family. Maybe she should change her mind about France. But then again, a dance career was so short. If she took time out now, she'd miss chances she couldn't afford to pass her by. She needed to be utterly dedicated to her job—and she had to hope that at some point in the future she could make it up to her sisters.

Holly's coin test was a good idea, though.

'Heads I'll do the show; tails I won't,' she said aloud, tossed the coin, and caught it on the back of her hand.

When she took the top hand off to reveal the coin showing tails, she discovered that her sister had been spot on. It really did tell her what she wanted…

Rory's phone pinged and Pippa's name flashed up on the screen at the top of the message.

Spoke to Nathalie. Happy to do piece about wasp. Twelve-thirty OK? What's the dress code? Pippa

He smiled and typed back.

Thank you. Twelve-thirty at the box office is fine. Dress code's whatever you feel comfortable wearing. Rory

He'd just sent the message when he remembered that she hadn't watched his show. He added swiftly:

Most people I interview wear whatever they normally wear at work.

She texted back.

Thank you. That's helpful. I'll bring lunch. Any (non-vespine) allergies or dietary stuff?

Oh, he liked those brackets. He liked *her*. And he was really looking forward to that interview.

He replied:

I eat anything.

And then he found himself typing:

Big weakness for brownies and scones.

No. That was steering into flirting territory. Except, instead of hitting the delete key, he accidentally hit the enter key. And it was too late to recall the message because she'd already read it.

Oh, great. How to make himself look foolish in her eyes.

He was about to type an apology when his phone pinged.

Noted.

And she'd added an emoji to tell him he'd just made her cry with laughter.

Ah, well. At least it'd make her relax with him instead of being nervous about being filmed. Then again, her job meant walking out onto a stage and performing in front of a sea of strangers; the chances were, she'd find filming an absolute breeze.

And that was another thing. He'd been so focused on seeing Pippa again that he'd completely forgotten about Kenise, his camerawoman. He texted Pippa again.

My camerawoman's vegetarian—I'll bring wraps for all of us.

Pippa replied.

OK. Then I'm in charge of pudding.

On Friday, Rory woke feeling as if life was getting back to normal again. He had interviews for his wasp piece scheduled during the day, his guests had all confirmed they would be there for the chat show section in the studio at five, and he'd sorted out the order of the other pieces he was going to use in the round-up. Busy, busy, busy—just how he liked it.

His mother was lying in wait in the kitchen. 'Eat some breakfast before you go,' she said. 'And if you're tired, you'll stop. Promise?'

There wasn't a way to stop her worrying— or was there? 'Thank you for looking after me, this week,' he said, giving her a hug. 'And nagging. You were right—I needed these few days off.' That wasn't strictly true, from his point of view, but he knew it would make his mother feel better. 'And now I'm ready to do the job I love again,' he said.

'And you'll let your father drive you to the studio?'

'No need. I'm going there after my last interview to do the voiceover and put the wasp piece together, then run through the first half of the show to check timings,' he said. 'I'm not going to make him turn out in rush-hour traffic. I was planning to get a taxi back afterwards—unless you wanted to come and sit in the audience for the live section, in which case I'll take you both out to dinner and we'll get a cab home afterwards.'

'That'd be nice,' Helena said.

'All right. I'll put your names on the list

with security, and I'll see you after the show,' he said.

He met Kenise, his camerawoman, at his GP's surgery for the interview; then they went to his godmother's house, where Kenise took various shots of the garden while he stayed in the kitchen, safely away from any wasps; he planned to add the voiceover in the studio. It was slightly unnerving to be back in the place where his heart had actually stopped beating; but at the same time he needed to face it and reassure Rosemary that he was absolutely fine.

Finally he headed to the Fitzroy Theatre. His first interview was with Nathalie Charrier to talk about the Fitzroy's upcoming gala show and the roof repairs; although he would've liked to get up on the roof to take a few shots, he thought that might be a step too far.

And then, at last, it was time to meet Pippa by the box office.

She was wearing leggings and a pretty T-shirt, as she had been yesterday, but today her hair was up in a bun and she definitely looked like an off-duty ballerina.

'Lovely to see you again, Pippa,' he said, shaking her hand and hoping it came across as professional. 'Pippa, this is Kenise, who does all my camerawork; Kenise, this is Pippa, the person who saved my life.'

'Good to meet you,' Kenise said, smiling broadly. 'Thank you for saving his life—and my job.'

'We all know you would've been snapped up within seconds,' Rory said, rolling his eyes and laughing.

'You said it would be about ten minutes of filming?' Pippa checked.

'Yes, though I won't use all of it on screen. I'll ask different questions, and you answer as if we're just having a chat. If you stop or mix your words up, that's fine. We can reshoot anything. I might stop and take a different angle, depending on what you say. Then I'll edit it together.'

'All right,' she said.

They went outside the theatre; Kenise took panning shots of the exterior of the theatre, then came to join them on the steps.

'I had no idea I was severely allergic to wasp stings until I was talking to ballerina Pippa Barnes at the garden party, while we were raising funds for the Fitzroy's roof,' Rory said. 'And I was incredibly lucky to be stung in front of someone who knew exactly how to save my life. Pippa, how did you know something was wrong and what to do next?'

'At ballet classes, one of my friends was severely allergic to almonds and accidentally ate some,' Pippa said. 'She collapsed in front of me, the same way that you did, so I realised you must be severely allergic to something.' She ran through what happened.

'Thanks to you, I'm here to tell the tale,' Rory said. 'What was going through your head when you did the CPR?'

'That I wanted to keep the blood pumping round your system until the paramedics came,' she answered honestly. 'It was pure instinct.'

He ran through the procedure again, this time asking slightly different questions and with Kenise taking a different camera angle.

'And that's everything I need,' he said at the end. 'Thank you.' He smiled. 'Shall we have lunch?'

'Sure. If you'd like to find a table, I'll get pudding from my locker,' Pippa said.

'She's lovely,' Kenise said as he ushered her into the restaurant area. 'I can see why you're smitten.'

'I'm not in the least bit smitten, Ken,' Rory protested. 'As I said to you earlier, she's articulate and she loves her subject. I'd really like her to do the show—but only if she's happy to do it.'

'I think she likes you, too,' Kenise said.

Rory sighed. 'I'm not looking for a relationship. She's busy with her career, and I'm busy with mine.'

'You picked a few girls who weren't right for you,' Kenise said. 'She's not like them—she doesn't treat you as a TV star or as royalty. She treats you as an equal.'

'You've worked with me for four years,' Rory said, 'and I love you dearly. But please don't try to matchmake. This is business.'

'If you say so,' Kenise said, hamming up her Jamaican accent and making it sound more like *I don't believe a word of it.*

Pippa joined them a couple of moments later, carrying a patisserie box. 'This is from the bakery round the corner from my flat,' she said.

'And these are from the deli round the corner from my parents,' Rory said, bringing out plain paper bags.

'What, no posh picnic hamper today?' Pippa teased.

'My first interview was at eight, this morning,' Rory said. 'So there wasn't time to pretty it up. Today there are chicken salad wraps— that's hummus and falafel for you, Ken, in a separate paper bag.'

'Gotta love a boss who pays attention to his team,' Kenise said with a grin.

'Have you two worked together very long?' Pippa asked.

'Long enough to finish—' Kenise began.

'—each other's sentences,' Rory said, laughing. 'What Ken doesn't know about film isn't worth knowing. She's taught me a lot.'

'You already knew a lot before I met you,' Kenise said. 'And he doesn't mansplain, so I can put up with him.'

'Sounds good,' Pippa said with a smile.

'I interviewed Nathalie this morning,' he said. 'About the Fitzroy's roof, and the gala.'

'Will that be going on tonight's show?' she asked.

'Yes. And she also gave us permission to do some filming in the dress rehearsal this afternoon,' he said. 'The one for the gala show, with you as the Sugar Plum Fairy. I'd like to film the whole piece, then pick a few seconds of footage to include in my introduction to you.'

She looked surprised. 'I—well, if Nathalie's said yes, then it's fine with me.'

'I have to cut the show together and do the guest spots this afternoon,' he said, 'so Nathalie's changing the order just for today—you'll do your piece first, so Kenise can film and we'll leave before the next performer comes on.'

'Then I'll be skipping pudding,' she said lightly, 'and you and Kenise can finish that box between you.'

'If you're sure, then thank you,' Rory said.

'No, *really* thank you,' Kenise said. 'I love brownies.'

'My pleasure,' Pippa said. Her phone alarm rang. 'My cue for work,' she said.

'See you on stage,' Rory said. 'And I'll talk to you next week about the series.'

'Sure. Nice to meet you, Kenise,' she said.

'She's really lovely,' Kenise said. 'Your parents would like her. And your sister. And your sister-in-law.'

'It's business,' Rory said, even though he agreed with her privately. But Pippa had made it clear that she was focused on her career; nothing was going to happen between them. Plus he wasn't taking the risk of messing up his documentary, by getting involved with the person he wanted to star in it. She was strictly off limits.

Nathalie came over to them. 'Ready to film?'

'Ready,' Rory said.

She led them into the auditorium; Kenise checked the lights and then got into the right position.

Rory had seen *The Nutcracker* several times over the years, and was very familiar with the music and the traditional routine; but even so he found himself spellbound when Pippa walked out onto the stage.

He'd last seen her wearing leggings and a pretty T-shirt. It had only been a few minutes ago—and yet here she was, completely transformed into the Queen of the Land of Sweets, a gilded crown on her head. Her dress was of the palest pink, and it seemed to shimmer underneath the lights; there were tiny star-shaped sequins sewn on the bodice, and the tutu was overlaid with gauze. And the way she moved, light as thistledown, gliding effortlessly across the stage in perfect timing with the eerie sound of the celestina…

Rory was completely transfixed.

He'd never seen the piece danced so beautifully—so perfectly.

Right at that very second he really could believe that she was a fairy. That last chain of pirouettes, the complicated footwork, the delicate movement of her tutu, the smile on her face…

As the final note died away, he stood up and clapped, unable to help himself. 'Brava,' he called.

She smiled, blew him a kiss, then walked gracefully off the stage—a fairy queen to the last.

CHAPTER FIVE

PIPPA HAD BEEN so aware of Rory sitting in the front row as she'd danced. She'd felt as if she'd been dancing just for him. And she'd loved every second of it, channelling the character of the fairy queen, her movements light and precise and in perfect timing with the music.

At the end, Rory had given her a standing ovation. He'd looked stunned, as if he hadn't expected her to dance quite like that. And he'd looked as if the magic of the piece had sprinkled its fairy dust on him, too. She hadn't been able to resist blowing him that kiss. And then, being a coward, she'd left the stage without looking to see his reaction.

If she was honest with herself, yes, she was attracted to him.

Which made the 'tails' bit of the coin test the sensible choice: she shouldn't do his show, because there was a huge risk that she might let him distract her from her goals. What if Rory became too much of a temptation? If she didn't get that promotion, then she'd be failing her parents all over again. She'd already disappointed them by choosing dance over medicine. Being a flop at her career wasn't an option. Doing Rory's show would be too much of a risk.

The problem was, she'd *wanted* that coin to land heads-up.

So did she follow her heart and do the show, or did she follow her common sense and turn him down?

The more she thought about it, the less she could answer.

Maybe she needed to let things settle in the back of her head for a bit longer.

Between rehearsals and the evening performance, Pippa texted her parents to let them know that she was going to be on Rory's show that evening, giving them the time and channel in case they wanted to see it. After chatting in the restroom with some of the other dancers, then a snack of a banana and an energy bar, she had her hair and make-up done, got changed into her costume and warmed up her muscles again, preparing to dance.

As always, the second that the curtain went up, the familiar adrenalin kicked in. Pippa loved the challenge of dancing the twin roles of heroine and villainess in the same show, portraying the emotional vulnerability of Odette and the seductive deception of Odile. And she hoped that just maybe she might inspire one young dancer in the audience, the way she'd been inspired at her own first visit to see *Swan Lake*.

On her way home after the show, she checked her phone; there were messages from her sisters and both her parents saying they'd seen her piece on Rory's show. Her sisters had said she looked as if she were flying when she danced, so light and delicate; her parents said how proud they were of her for saving Rory's life.

Well, of course her parents would focus on the medical side of things, she thought wryly. The life they still felt she should've had.

But then her mother had added, *'You dance so beautifully.'* Which made Pippa feel as if her mother, at least, was finally starting to understand how much her career meant to her. Maybe one day she would stop feeling that she'd let them down. Though, that didn't mean she had room in her life for a relationship. How could she prioritise romance over the thing that made her who she was? She'd only end up letting a partner down as much as she'd let her family down.

Back at her flat, she made herself a mug of camomile tea, heated up the pasta dish she'd prepped earlier, and found Rory's show on the catch-up section of the arts channel. She curled up on the sofa and ate dinner while she watched. His piece about the wasp stings was excellent, but she really enjoyed the piece on the Fitzroy, with Nathalie talking about the gala and how they'd be dancing favourite ballet pieces, from traditional classical works through to more modern choreography.

She could see how Rory had edited the bits he'd filmed with her to help tell the story effectively. He'd used several short clips of her dancing, and ended the section about the Fitzroy gala with Pippa's last few pirouettes in the 'Dance of the Sugar Plum Fairy'. She was used to practising in a studio with a mirror, so she could check she was happy with any particular pose or move, but seeing herself dancing on screen felt very different—almost as if she was watching someone else. She was relieved to note that the clip was technically flawless.

The final section was the chat show, and she loved the way Rory drew his guests out. He had a real knack for putting people at their ease, and it was more like watching old friends having a good chat than a formal interview.

At the end, she messaged him.

I enjoyed your show.

A moment later, her phone pinged with a return message.

Thank you. I enjoyed your Sugar Plum Fairy.

Thank you. I'll be watching your show in future.

I'm definitely getting a ticket for the Fitzroy gala show. What did you dance tonight?

Swan Lake. Though dancers don't necessarily play the same part every night.

Why not?

That message was rapidly followed by:

Can I call you?

Sure.

Her phone rang.

'Hey. I know you're working tomorrow, so I won't keep you long,' Rory promised. 'Tell me about *Swan Lake*.'

'Tonight I danced Odette/Odile,' she said, 'but some nights I dance as one of the Two Swans in Acts Two and Four, and other nights I dance as one of the Prince's sisters.'

'Why don't you dance the same part every night?' he asked.

'Because some parts—like Odette/Odile—really take it out of you,' she explained. 'A dancer risks burnout if they dance a major part every single night. Plus you need several people in every performance who can cover different parts, in case someone's taken ill at the last minute or has a family crisis and can't make a show. Besides, it's good for dancers to learn a mix of parts, so they can extend their range and repertoire.' She paused, realising that he hadn't said a thing. 'Sorry. I can get a bit boring about dance.'

'You're not boring,' he said. 'I'm being quiet because I'm making notes. These are the kinds of points I'd like to cover in the series—which isn't me pressuring you to say yes, it's just you've given me something really interesting to think about, and probably a ton of questions.'

'Oh.' He wasn't bored, then. Funny how that made her feel warm inside.

'Do you dance every night?' he asked.

'It depends on the cast. Sometimes I have a night off during the week, though I normally come in and watch the performance from the wings.' Then it occurred to her that it might not be what he'd meant. 'We don't have shows on

Sunday or Monday, so that's the equivalent of the weekend for me.'

'I hadn't really thought about that, but you work Friday and Saturday nights,' he mused. 'Of course your "weekend" wouldn't be the same as it is for someone in an office job.'

'It's all part of working in the arts,' she said. 'Musicians on tour have a lot of travelling in between shows, and they might be working ten or fourteen days in a row, depending on what their promoters book. And you probably work unusual hours.'

'Well, yes,' he said. 'But it doesn't matter, because I love my job.'

'Me, too,' she said.

'Well, I'm glad you enjoyed my show,' he said. 'No pressure, but I'll wait to hear from you about whether you'll do the ballet documentary with me. I've already got a yes from the tango expert.'

'And John Travolta for the disco?' she couldn't help teasing.

'Sadly, my mum's going to miss out on that one. But, yes, I have a disco dancer arranged.' She could practically hear the smile in his voice. 'Plus a tango expert and a ballroom specialist.'

'OK. Speak to you soon,' she said.

The next morning, in the middle of the conditioning class, it occurred to Pippa that Rory could shadow her for a few days. If he took part in the warm-up, he could experience the exercises for himself; and although he wouldn't be doing any actual dancing, he could at least see how rehearsals worked. Maybe the wardrobe team could fit him for a costume and do stage hair and make-up, too. Obviously he'd be used to make-up for the chat show segment of his TV show, but stage make-up was very different and it could be fun.

At the break between class and rehearsals, she went to find Nathalie. 'I was thinking— could Rory maybe shadow me at work for a few days?' she asked. 'Not all the time, obviously, but enough so he gets an idea of how things fit together to make a performance and what goes on behind the scenes?'

'You've decided to do the show, then?' Nathalie asked.

'*Nearly* decided.' She just needed to banish those last niggling doubts. 'But it would be useful background for him, even if I don't do the show.'

'He'll only be observing, not filming?' Nathalie checked.

'Observing, and maybe doing the conditioning class, if Kenzo doesn't mind. It wouldn't be fair to anyone to put him in a rehearsal class, when he doesn't have a clue what a tendu is or what "fifth position arms" means,' Pippa said, 'because either we'd have to stop and show him what to do, or he'd try to follow us and get in a muddle.'

'I'll talk to Kenzo about it,' Nathalie said. 'If Rory gets to a point where he wants to film anyone other than you, then everyone needs to agree to it. And they need credits on the programme.'

'Of course,' Pippa said. 'Thank you, Nathalie.'

Before the rehearsals started, she texted Rory.

Talked to Nathalie. She says you can shadow me here, watch the classes and rehearsals, and maybe take the conditioning class.

Her phone rang almost immediately. 'Is now a good time for you to talk?'

'I've got about three minutes,' she said.

'OK. Are you busy on Sunday?' he asked.

Why? Was he going to ask her out? All her nerve-ends started to tingle. If he did…what if she gave in to the temptation to say yes?

'Just catching up with chores,' she said carefully.

'Maybe we could meet up, if you have time. I can answer any questions you might have about the dance show.'

He hadn't been asking her on a date, then:

this was work. And how ridiculous that she felt disappointed. After all, hadn't she been telling herself that she didn't want him to distract her? And she had nothing to offer him anyway. Dance always came first, even before her family. How could she even consider committing to a relationship, when it was obvious that her partner would have to take second place to her career? She'd end up letting him down, the same way she'd let her family down.

Even if she could get past that, there was the fact that they'd be working together. It really wouldn't be appropriate to have a relationship with him. He was off limits.

'I haven't quite made my decision, yet,' she said. Which wasn't strictly true; she'd made the decision, but she was having an uncharacteristic wobble about it. Normally, she knew exactly what her next move would be, where her career was concerned, but something about Rory raised all the doubts she'd suppressed over the years.

'Or we could just meet up for a coffee,' he said. 'I would suggest going for a walk in the park, but I'd hate for you to have to save my life all over again.'

She ought to tell him she was too busy to see him. But her mouth seemed to have other ideas. 'We could go for an indoor walk,' she said. 'Maybe in a museum or a gallery?'

'That would be great. Where would you like to go?'

She'd done it, now. 'Somewhere easy to get to—how about the National Gallery?'

'OK. I'll meet you by the entrance at...when's good for you?'

She usually slept in a little later on Sundays. 'Eleven?'

'Eleven it is. I'll see you then.'

The warmth in Rory's voice made her feel warm all over, too. But she made herself concentrate and not think of him at all during rehearsals.

On her lunch break, she looked him up properly—telling herself it was just because she wanted to know more about him if she was going to work with him. There seemed to be a lot of pictures of him on social media, at parties with gorgeous actresses and models; clearly he lived a glamorous life.

She skimmed over the words, then stopped dead and backtracked. The *Honourable* Rory Fanshawe? Hang on... Did that mean he was minor royalty or something?

A couple more clicks, and she discovered that Rory was the youngest son of the Earl and Countess of Riverford.

But he'd introduced himself to her as Rory Fanshawe, not as Lord Whatever-He-Was. Though being blue-blooded would explain his accent and his knowledge of Latin, which tended to be taught more in private schools than state schools.

A little more research told her that he'd gone to Eton, as had his older brother; his sister had gone to a private day school.

They were from totally different worlds. Worlds that she didn't think would fit well together. How would his family ever think her enough for him? Surely they'd expect him to end up with someone born into the aristocracy—someone who understood that way of life? She wasn't enough for her parents because she hadn't gone into medicine; she wasn't a good enough sister because she let dancing get in the way of keeping in touch; and if she wasn't good enough to make Principal Dancer it would all have been for nothing. Risking a relationship with Rory and failing that, too— that was one step too far.

So the ridiculous thoughts that had been starting to form in her brain would just have to be ignored. There was no chance of anything romantic developing between them. She and Rory might become friends, but no more than that.

In a way, she thought, finding out the truth about his background had done her a favour. Knowing that nothing would happen between them meant that she could do the show without being distracted by him.

On Sunday, Pippa headed out to meet Rory in Trafalgar Square. The area was already busy with people snapping pictures of Nelson's column and the lions, and children watching the fountains.

Rory was waiting for her by the entrance to the National Gallery, as they'd arranged, and together they went into the main hall.

'Shall we start with the oldest ones and work forwards?' he asked. 'Or can I take you to see my favourite painting here?'

What would the son of an earl like most? she wondered. Something very traditional? Or something that kicked against the traces?

'Show me your favourite,' she said.

It turned out to be one of the more modern pieces in the gallery: a woman in a room, with her back to the artist.

'*Interior*, by Vilhelm Hammershøi,' she said, reading the notes next to the painting. 'I'm sorry, I've never heard of him.'

'He's one of the Danish Symbolists,' he said. 'This is a painting of his wife in their house in

Copenhagen. I like it because we only see her back, so whatever she's thinking or doing is a complete mystery to whoever's looking at the painting—and that means whatever you think the painting means.'

She looked at him. 'And *that* never occurred to me, either. Did you study History of Art at uni?'

'English Literature,' he said with a smile. 'I've learned a bit about art from the curators I've talked to over the years. I wrote an article for an internet magazine about Hammershøi's work, a couple of years back. *Dust Motes with Sunbeams* is the painting I really fell in love with.' He took his phone from his pocket, tapped on the screen and brought up a painting to show her. Winter sunlight shone diagonally through a window in the centre of a room, illuminating particles of dust and throwing patterns of light and shade on the floor. 'The light's the connection between the inside and the outside,' he said.

'I can see why you like it,' she said. 'It's lovely. Almost like a photograph.'

'And this one,' he said, shepherding her over to a painting of a lake among mountains, the water whipped into zigzags by the wind. 'Again, it's the light and the colour palette that draws me in.'

'Basically you like Scandi art?' she asked, peering at the description by the painting and discovering that the artist, Akseli Gallen-Kallela, was Finnish.

'I do,' he said with a grin. 'Lottie—my sister—teases me about *hygge* all the time. But I really like the clean lines and the lightness of Scandinavian style.'

Which was a million miles away from the huge dark paintings found in stately homes—or the acres of gilding. 'I kind of expected you to be a big fan of Reynolds and all the royal portrait painters,' she said.

He frowned. 'Why?'

'I looked you up,' she said. 'You never said your dad was an earl.'

At least he had the grace to wince. 'Ah. That.'

'Should I be calling you Lord Fanshawe?' she asked.

'No. I'm the younger son so I'm plain Mr. Though I get a courtesy title to use on paper,' he added.

'That's the "honourable" bit?'

'Yes, though I don't use it at work. My brother Jamie is the heir apparent, so he gets one of Dad's other titles. He's Viscount Allingham.' He sighed. 'I *did* tell you I had a privileged up-bringing.'

She remembered; she'd misinterpreted it at

the time. Though he hadn't enlightened her, either. 'I didn't realise you meant you were part of the aristocracy.'

For a moment, he tensed. Then he said, 'It's honestly not that big a deal.'

She wasn't so sure. Why was he sensitive about her asking about his upbringing? Maybe she should be kind and back off; but she was curious. Really curious. 'Isn't it? I mean—you must know the royal family.'

'I do, but only in the same way that say a teacher would have a lot of teacher friends, or you have a lot of dancer friends. It's only part of my life. That's why I didn't mention it before,' he explained. 'It honestly isn't a big deal. This isn't the Regency era; my parents aren't snobs who look down on people who haven't been born into privilege. Neither of my in-laws come from the aristocracy.'

She bit her lip. 'Sorry. I didn't mean to accuse your family of being snobbish.' And her earlier thought about her social class being a barrier between them—well, it wasn't.

'I'm probably being oversensitive,' he said. 'Because I hate it when people see me as a posh boy trading on my dad's connections. I did think about using a stage name for my broadcasting work, but then I realised it'd be a bit pointless because it'd only take a couple of clicks on a search engine to find out who my dad is. But I got my job because of what I can do, not because of my name.'

It sounded as if people had accused him of that before. She wasn't surprised that rankled, because from what she'd seen he put a lot of work into his show. In his shoes, she'd be a bit sensitive about it, too.

'I just want to be seen for who I am—as a person,' he said.

'I can understand that,' she said. 'I suppose it's like the children of rock stars or actors— they might want to follow in their parents' footsteps because they love music or acting. But, however hard they work, people will still think they only got their first break because of who their parents are.'

'Exactly,' he said. 'The society rags call me a prime catch because I'm the son of the Earl of Riverford, and I loathe it. Marriage shouldn't be about seeing someone as a fish to be reeled in— it should be because you're attracted to someone and you like spending time with them.' His face darkened. 'And I hate it when women flirt with me because they think I can get into them into TV.'

Pippa was shocked. 'You think that's why women date you—because you could be a good connection for them?'

'Put it this way, I don't seem to be very good at picking someone who sees me for myself,' he said.

And she'd pretty much asked him questions that made it sound as if she was just like his exes, interested in his connections rather than in him. 'I'm sorry,' she said. 'I didn't mean to trample on a sore spot.'

'It's fine.' He blew out a breath. 'Just sometimes it gets to me. I mean—I'm twenty-nine. My brother and sister were both married by the time they were my age. They both had children. They were *settled*. And here I am, racketing around.'

'Is that what you're looking for? A life partner and children?' she asked carefully.

If that was what he really wanted, it was something she couldn't give him. Not without giving up her career, which she wasn't prepared to do; or asking him to wait for so many years that her fertility would be on the wane, which wouldn't be fair to him.

'No. Yes. I don't know.' He shook his head. 'Everything was a lot clearer before the wasp issue. I was taking a year or so out of dating to concentrate on my career and get a bit closer to where I want to go next,' he said. 'But, this past week, my family's wrapped me in cotton wool and I've had nothing to do except think.'

He grimaced. 'I felt as if I was sleepwalking, in hospital. Stuck behind a wall and I couldn't get out.'

'To be fair, they did need to keep an eye on you, in case you had another reaction,' Pippa said.

'I know,' he said. 'But living in my head hasn't been good for me. I thought I knew where my life was going, but now it feels as if I'm lost in a maze full of briars. I've been reassessing everything and it's made me wonder: am I letting my family down?'

Oh, she knew that one well. *Really* well. He had her complete sympathies.

'I feel like the spoiled, selfish baby who doesn't seem to stick to anything and always dates Ms Wrong,' he finished.

'You don't come across as a spoiled baby,' she said. 'I wouldn't presume to lecture you about your love life, but you've clearly stuck to your career. If you couldn't do your job well, you wouldn't get decent ratings and you would've been replaced by now, with someone who'd bring in the viewers and more advertising money.'

'I wasn't fishing for compliments,' he said, 'but thank you. Looking at it that way helps.'

'What you said about feeling that you've let your family down?' She gave him a wry smile.

'That makes two of us.' She grimaced. 'And I know we're supposed to be talking about your dance series, but that bit's not for public consumption and I'd rather you didn't include it in your show.'

'Noted. And you can trust me,' he said. 'Apart from the fact that I keep my word, if you said anything to the press about what I just told you, they'd have a field day.'

He had a point: he was as vulnerable to gossip as she was. Maybe more so, because television had a much wider reach than a ballet stage. 'This stays between you and me,' she said. Which felt strangely intimate. She'd just told him things she hadn't told anyone else; and she had the feeling that he'd confided in her in just the same way. They were almost strangers; yet there was a connection between them. Maybe it was because he'd been so close to death and she'd been so instrumental in saving his life, but she felt oddly close to him.

'Why do you think you've let your family down?' he asked. 'You're doing really well in your career.'

'I'm the only one in three generations of my family not to be a doctor,' she said. 'I chose ballet over medical school.'

'If you have a talent, surely it's a waste to ignore it and do something else just because everyone else in your family does?' Rory asked.

'Maybe,' she said. 'But, because I didn't take a conventional route into ballet, I always feel that I have to work twice as hard as everyone else, even to prove that I have the same kind of commitment.'

'That's why you're so focused on getting promoted?'

She nodded. 'It'll show everyone that I made the right career choice.' Including herself: maybe then she'd feel that she was good enough to do her job, not an imposter.

'You're doing what you love,' he said. 'That tells me you've made the right choice. Would you be happy, being a doctor?'

'I don't know,' she said. 'But sometimes I think maybe I should've followed the career path my parents planned for me. At least as a doctor I'd be doing something important. Helping people.'

'As a dancer, you're helping people,' Rory said. 'The arts are food for the soul. A world without music, without paintings, without theatre and dance—where's the joy?'

'That's what your programme's about, isn't it?' she asked. 'Sharing the joy.'

He nodded. 'I know what you mean, though. Sometimes I feel as if I'm frivolous. Not the showbiz parties—there aren't anywhere near as many of those as the press likes to make out, and they're not my idea of a good time anyway—but the arts are so often seen as a luxury. They're the first thing to go when money's tight and bills need to be paid.'

'Except maybe they're more than a luxury,' she said. 'The arts are about your mental health. Like you said—it's about the joy. And maybe seeing something on your show will persuade the audience to try doing it themselves. Dancing's so good for taking you out of a tough place. When you're counting steps and you have to concentrate on what your arms and legs are doing, you don't have the headspace to think about your worries. Even if it's only for half an hour, that tiny break from worrying can give you the strength to carry on.'

'It's the same when you're watching a film, or reading, or wandering round an art gallery and telling yourself the story behind the picture—it's like a step out of your real life that helps you put a bit of space between you and your worries, and it means you can cope.' He paused. 'We're on the same side, Pippa.'

'I think we are,' she agreed.

'Let's walk and look at some more paintings,' he said, and she walked with him towards the Impressionists' room. 'I know I said I wasn't going to pressure you—but I think you'd be perfect for my series. You love your job and you're good at explaining what you do.' He paused. 'So what's holding you back from saying yes?'

CHAPTER SIX

FOR A MOMENT, Pippa looked haunted, and Rory was about to back off when she said, 'If you really want to know, I worry that doing your show is going to distract me. I can't allow *anything* to sidetrack me. My parents don't understand why I never date, and my sisters are always nagging me not to work so hard—but I *have* to. I don't have *time* to date. If I lose my focus at work, I'll lose my chance of being promoted. And that promotion's really important to me.'

She'd said it would prove to her parents that she'd made the right career choice. Perhaps, he thought, she needed that proof for herself, too. To show her that all the sacrifices she'd made were worth it.

'Or maybe you could see the documentary as a safety net,' he said. 'There's a pretty good chance that the management team of other ballet companies will be watching it. They'll see you dancing, but more importantly they'll see how you come across on screen. If Nathalie doesn't give you the promotion, I reckon you'll get calls from people interested in you joining their companies as a Principal Dancer.'

'Maybe,' she said. 'Though I like working at the Fitzroy. It's the first company that gave me a chance—and it feels like home. I don't want to leave.'

Rory understood exactly what she meant. If he wanted to climb the ladder, eventually he'd need to move on from the company that had given him the chance to hone his skills; he'd still miss his team and their camaraderie. 'You won't get distracted,' he said.

She didn't look as if she believed him.

And then the penny dropped. That pull he'd felt towards her—did she feel it, too? His mouth went dry. Was *he* the reason she was holding back?

The words slipped out before he could stop them. 'Do you think *I'm* going to distract you?'

Her face coloured. 'Yes,' she muttered.

Now he got it. And, now he thought about it, he had a feeling that she could distract him, too. 'Don't worry. You're perfectly safe with me,' he said, 'I'm not looking for a relationship.' At least, he didn't want the kind of relationship he'd fallen into for the last three or four years, where his girlfriends hadn't seen him for who he was inside. 'The same way that I'm safe with you, because you're obviously not looking for a relationship, either—plus you see past me being the youngest son of the Earl of Riverford or being a TV presenter.'

She frowned. 'But you just told me your series could help my career.'

'As a ballerina, or at least give you options elsewhere if Nathalie doesn't promote you,' he said. 'That isn't the same thing as helping you get a start in TV.' She wouldn't be using him for his connections, the way his exes had; but dating her would be a mistake. She'd been very clear that she didn't have the time or space in her life for a relationship. Which meant anything that might happen between them had no future. What was the point in setting himself up for more hurt?

'I suppose—'

But, before she could continue, a middle-aged woman came over to them, and asked, 'Rory Fanshawe? It *is* you, isn't it?'

'Yes,' he said.

She beamed at him. 'I told my husband it was you. He said I was being a silly old fool.' She turned to Pippa. 'I'm so sorry to interrupt your date, my dear. But I wanted to tell Rory how much I enjoyed his show. I watch it every week without fail.' She turned back to Rory and smiled again. 'If it wasn't for you telling us about it, I would've missed that wonderful exhibition of the Pre-Raphaelites the other month.'

'That's good to hear. I hope you enjoyed it,' Rory said, smiling back at her.

'I did—very much. I just wanted to thank you,' she said. 'I'll let you get on with your day.'

'Thank you. And it was lovely to meet you,' Rory said, shaking her hand.

'Does that happen very often?' Pippa asked quietly when the woman was out of earshot. 'People coming up to you when you're out?'

'It's becoming more frequent,' Rory admitted. 'But, actually, that's the best bit of my job—hearing from a viewer that I've shared something they've really enjoyed. That my work's made a difference. I'm always happy to talk to fans. Without them, I wouldn't have a job.' He looked at her. 'Don't people come up to you?'

'Outside the Fitzroy? Not really. Apart from ballet-goers, most people wouldn't know who I am,' she said. 'Though that isn't an issue. I'm just happy being able to do what I love.' She paused. 'So what's your game plan?'

'I'm still working that out,' Rory said. 'I love the format of my show. I like meeting new people, and I think one of my strengths is getting people to open up to me. What I do in the arts round-up is halfway between commercial tele-vision and the more formal documentaries that the critics like. I'd like to think there's a way I can keep doing both. I enjoy the commercial stuff with a broader audience that persuades people to look at something they might other-wise miss, but I want to do serious arts docu-mentaries as well—to go into more depth with things than I can in my show right now.'

'Your dance series is the first step towards that—pun not intended,' she added.

He chuckled. 'But it works very nicely.' He looked at her. 'You're the first person I've told about any of this.'

'Even though we're practically strangers.'

'Maybe that makes it easier,' Rory said. 'We don't have any expectations of how each other will react.' He paused. 'What's your game plan, then? Apart from becoming Principal Dancer?'

'I've got maybe ten years left dancing on stage in a lead role,' Pippa said. 'After that, it's either playing character roles—say, Juliet's nurse in *Romeo and Juliet* or Carabosse in *The Sleeping Beauty*—or teaching. Or maybe cho-reography. But Principal Dancer is at least my five-year plan.'

Even though she didn't quite believe in her-self, she'd planned her career and she'd work hard enough to get where she wanted, Rory thought. 'That sounds good,' he said.

His hand brushed against hers accidentally as they walked through the gallery, and it felt as if he'd been galvanised. He didn't dare look at her to gauge her reaction, and instead pretended it hadn't happened. He kept the conversation light and focused on the art, and discovered that she liked paintings full of sunshine—and, of course, Degas' ballet dancers.

But, as they moved through the rooms, he found himself really aware of her; sometimes, when they stood looking at a painting and talking, they were close enough that he could feel the warmth of her skin and smell the sweet vanilla scent of her perfume. Even though he was trying to concentrate on being professional, he found himself wondering what it would be like if this was a real date. What it would be like to hold her hand. How it would feel to hold her close. How her mouth would feel against his…

It had been a while since he'd felt a pull like this towards someone. And he knew he needed to suppress it: she'd already said she didn't want to get distracted from her career. Despite his good intentions to say goodbye and leave her to think about whether she would do his show, his mouth had other ideas, because he said, 'Can I buy you lunch? Not with strings—just because it's my turn.' And because he really wasn't ready to say goodbye to her just yet.

'Thank you. That'd be nice.' Her smile was open and honest, and it made him feel as if his heart had just done a backflip. Which was crazy. He wasn't supposed to be thinking about her in those terms.

They queued up in the café; she chose a goat's cheese, spinach and red pepper quiche with a green superfood salad.

'That looks so good. I think I'll have the same,' he said.

'So what's your favourite ballet?' he asked when they'd found a table, wanting to keep her talking to him, and guessing that her job was her favourite subject.

'To dance or to watch?' she asked.

'Both,' he said.

'*Swan Lake* to watch,' she said promptly. 'Whether it's the version with the scary all-male swans, or the absolute precision of a traditional version with the cygnets in tiaras and tutus. I love the music and the routines—and it always, always makes me cry.'

'Ballets are always tragedies, aren't they?' he asked. '*Swan Lake*, they both die; *Romeo and Juliet*, they both die; *Giselle*, they both die.'

'Actually,' she said,' there's a version of *Swan Lake* with a happy ending, where Prince Siegfried fights Rothbart and pulls off his wing, and that takes the enchantment off the swans, and he marries Odette.'

'It's nice to know that a happy ending's possible,' he said, 'but then how would it work with the music?'

'I don't have an answer for that one, because I've never seen that version,' she admitted. 'But tragedies aren't just in ballet. It's in opera, too—*Madame Butterfly, Tosca, La Traviata*. And everyone dies in Shakespeare's tragedies.'

'But there's comic opera—things like *The Marriage of Figaro*,' he said. 'And Shakespeare also wrote comedies.'

'There's a ballet version of *A Midsummer Night's Dream*,' she said. 'And there are other ballets with happy endings: *Sleeping Beauty* and the *Nutcracker*.'

'OK. I'll give you that,' he said. 'What about your favourite ballet to dance?'

'To be fair, it's whatever we're doing right now. I always find something new in a performance, even when it's a role I've danced before,' she said. 'I really loved doing *Cinderella*, last year. We had a different perspective—Cinderella was loved by the stepmother, but the stepsisters teased her by throwing her scarf around and she got upset about it being lost. When her dad went back to find it, he was accidentally killed by hunters. The stepmother was lost in grief and couldn't bear to have Cinderella around as a reminder of why her husband died.'

'That's definitely a different take on the fairy tale,' he said. 'And I like that. A motive that's stronger than just money.' He rolled his eyes. 'And yes, I know, that's rich coming from my background.'

'A double pun—very clever,' she said.

He inclined her head in acknowledgement. 'Which role did you dance?'

'Cinderella,' she said. 'And the bit I loved was my transformational dress.'

'What's that, in layman's terms?'

'It's a little bit of stage magic. In the first act, I wear a peasant dress. About half an hour into the show, I'm offstage for three minutes, and that's when I change into the transformational dress—it looks like the peasant dress on the outside, but there's a ballgown underneath,' she explained.

'You can change a costume in less than three minutes?' He could feel his eyes widening. He hadn't known that was possible.

'The wardrobe, hair and make-up department are extraordinary,' she said. 'It happens in opera and plays, too—they all work together at the same time, at amazing speeds.'

'So how does the dress work?' he asked. 'Don't the audience notice there are two dresses?'

'No. As I said, Wardrobe's amazing. It's all about the material they use and how they roll it to hide one dress under the other, sort of in a pocket. I pull a secret ring to unravel the stitching, then do some pirouettes,' she told him. 'The movement makes the peasant dress drop down and act as the underskirt to the ball-gown—which unfurls and swishes round me. The coach takes me to the ball, and that's when I change out of the transformational dress into the proper ballgown.'

'That's really clever.' And he liked the fact that he learned new things, with her. 'Though have you just broken a rule—you know, like magicians are supposed not to tell anyone how they do their tricks?'

'No, because even when you know how it's done it still looks amazing and you can believe in the magic,' she said. 'On the nights I wasn't dancing, I'd sit and watch it from the wings because it's just astonishing. There's probably a video about it on YouTube, if you wanted to look it up.'

'I think I need to include the make-up and wardrobe departments in the show,' he said. 'And I love the sound of that transformation scene. Do you think Nathalie would agree to let me film you dancing that piece?'

'You'd have to ask her,' Pippa said.

'So what happens in a normal day, as a ballet dancer?' he asked.

'Classes—stretching and conditioning, then technical—followed by rehearsals. Nathalie's agreed that you can observe and I was thinking, it might be useful for you to do the stretching class, to get a feel for what it's like. I talked to Kenzo, our physical development lead, and he said you can come along.'

'Thanks. Let me check my diary,' Rory said, and took out his phone. 'You have Mondays off, so I'm assuming the next class is Tuesday. What time?'

'Nine, and Kenzo's very hot on punctuality,' she said.

'Got it,' he said. 'What happens in technical classes?'

'Barre work to start, then combinations in the centre, then the big jumps.'

'The ones where I wonder if they've secretly got a trampoline in the floor, because how can you humanly jump that high and move your legs so fast?' he checked.

She chuckled, and he noticed how her eyes crinkled at the corners. Almost like rays of sun, he thought.

'It takes a lot of practice,' she said. 'People dip in and out of rehearsals, depending on what their role is. After lunch, it's more rehearsals, maybe a break, and then the show.'

'So basically you're at the theatre from nine in the morning until after the show at night, either rehearsing or dancing? Those are seriously long days,' he said.

'But it's my choice to do it.' She shrugged. 'It's just how it is. I love what I do. I catch up with family and friends on the phone, and I get to see them on Sundays, if they're free—as doctors, my family all work unsociable hours, too.'

Guilt flooded through him. 'Sorry. I didn't mean to take up so much of your free time today—especially now I know it's so limited.'

'I didn't have anything planned today,' she said, 'or I would've said I was busy and suggested talking to you another time.'

'I appreciate you making time for me.'

'No problem.' She smiled. 'Now you know what my day-to-day life is like as a dancer, tell me about life as a television star.'

'It's probably easier to show you,' he said. 'Maybe you could shadow me when I do an interview, so you get an idea of what happens and the sort of thing I'd ask you, if you want to be part of the series,' he added hastily. 'And then

I can show you how I edit the footage—how I decide what to include and what to leave out.'

'I take it you plan your questions before you do the interview?' she asked.

He nodded. 'I try to get a feel for my subject's background so I've got an idea of the kind of questions I want to ask, but they're more of a guide than something rigid. I try to let my subject lead and tell me things in their own words, because they're the expert,' he said. 'I'm looking forward to tomorrow's interview, because it's with a film score composer, Judith Parrish. She's only in her mid-twenties, and it's still quite rare to have a woman composing for films. Which is crazy,' he added, 'when you look at female pop stars and how many of them write their own songs.'

'What kind of films does she write for?' Pippa asked.

'She's written the score for a new version of *Persuasion*. I want to talk to her about that—what inspires her, how she approaches developing a score, what kind of research she does before she starts composing and how she structures it,' he said, He looked thoughtfully at her. 'If you decide to choreograph, later, maybe she'd be a good contact for you. Say, in developing a brand-new ballet.'

'I hadn't thought about that before,' she said.

'Developing something completely new. A new story, to new music and new routines, instead of reworking the classics.'

'Is that what you'd want to do in the future?' he asked.

'Maybe. That could be my plan for years ten to fifteen,' she said. And there was a light behind her eyes he hadn't seen before. Something new, something magical—perhaps even a dream so new she hadn't shared it with anyone else.

'Maybe she could write some pieces for your dance series, if you wanted new choreography,' she said.

Rory loved the idea of working with Pippa to create something completely new—and he told himself it was nothing to do with wanting to spend more time with her, and everything to do with developing his career towards producing critically acclaimed documentaries. 'Maybe. How long does it take to choreograph a new piece?' he asked.

'It depends on how long you want the piece to be, and whether it's a solo or for several dancers,' Pippa said. 'Choreographing's the quick bit. Teaching it to the dancers takes longer.'

Something was buzzing in his brain, something that felt like the light he'd seen in her eyes. Was it the excitement of new possibilities—or was it *her*, making him feel so different?

'If you're not doing anything else, you could come to Camden with me tomorrow and meet Judith,' he said impulsively.

'Won't she mind?'

'I'll call her this evening and check. But I'll tell her you're shadowing me because I'm hoping to work with you on another project. Plus, you work in the arts so you understand the importance of confidentiality.'

'All right,' she said, and it felt as if the sun had lit up the whole room—which, he thought, was totally crazy, considering that they were indoors and it was raining outside.

'Thank you. And I guess I've taken up enough of your Sunday,' he said.

'I do have a pile of laundry waiting for me,' she admitted. 'Though I've enjoyed today.'

'Me, too.' He wanted to linger, but he didn't want to scare her away.

'I'll see you tomorrow.'

'I'll check with Judith and text you the details later this evening,' he said. 'If she says yes, then I'll meet you at Camden Tube station at half-past nine.'

'OK. I'll wait to hear from you.'

He resisted the impulse to kiss her goodbye—it wasn't appropriate, and he wasn't supposed to be thinking about her in those terms—and instead watched her walk through the crowd. The way she moved, so graceful and sure, drew him. And he'd enjoyed talking with her; instead of sticking to social small talk, he'd been able to talk to her about something deeper, the kind of things he didn't usually share.

Pippa Barnes intrigued him. Maybe spending more time with her would help him shake off this weird sense of being hemmed in, which he'd been feeling ever since he'd got out of hospital. And maybe he could return the favour by making her see that she'd made the right choice in becoming a ballet dancer.

CHAPTER SEVEN

ON MONDAY MORNING, Rory was waiting outside the Tube station at Camden—making sure that he was well away from litter bins, the florist's stall, and anything else likely to attract wasps.

'Morning, sunshine,' Kenise said, walking up to him. 'Ready to go?'

'No. We need to wait for Pippa,' Rory said.

'Pippa?' Kenise raised her eyebrows. 'Why?'

'She's shadowing me today,' Rory explained. 'Just as I'm shadowing her tomorrow, though we're not actually filming—it's preliminary research.'

'Ri-i-i-ight,' Kenise said, sounding completely unconvinced.

'If she sees how I work, it might make her more relaxed about agreeing to do the show—and shadowing her will be helpful background for me,' Rory said.

'You're not doing this with any of the other dancers,' Kenise pointed out.

'Of course I am,' he said. 'I'm using the same structure for all the episodes: looking at the history of dance, famous dancers of the past, and then a day in the life of a modern dancer. We're filming them performing, and doing a video diary of them teaching me a routine.'

'But Pippa's the only one shadowing you,' Kenise said.

'She saved my life. I owe her.'

Kenise scoffed. 'Sounds to me like you're trying to find a good excuse. You really like her, don't you?'

Yes. And it was all a mess in his head. She'd made it clear she didn't want to get involved with anyone. How stupid would it be to let himself fall for someone who was unavailable? Almost as stupid as it had been to let himself fall for women who didn't see who he really was inside.

Except he thought Pippa *did* see him for exactly who he was. And that made her even more tempting.

'It's irrelevant,' he said. 'She's not looking for a relationship and neither am I.'

'You're protesting a bit too much, sweetie,' Kenise said.

He knew that. And he rather thought he was trying to convince himself as much as he was trying to convince Kenise. 'We're probably going to be colleagues. Which puts her completely off limits, because I don't want to risk making a mess of this documentary. Writing, presenting and producing: it's my chance to take the next step in my career, build myself up as someone people take seriously. Open some doors for me.'

'But you still like her.'

The worry must've shown on his face, because Kenise patted his shoulder. 'Don't worry. I'm not going to say anything in front of her.'

'Thank you,' he said.

'But if you're serious about the documentary, you need to focus on that and put your feelings for her to the side—at least for now,' Kenise said.

Which was pretty much how Pippa was approaching her chance for promotion, Rory thought. Work came first, second and last. Until last week, he wouldn't have had a problem with that, either. But then he'd nearly died, and it had changed him. Made him determined to live life to its fullest—to want everything. That made it hard for him to ignore the attraction he felt towards Pippa, even though he could come up with plenty of reasons why he should keep her at a distance. And he wasn't used to feeling so conflicted. 'Yeah,' he said. 'Let me take your camera.'

'I appreciate your gentlemanly concern, but I can manage,' Kenise said.

'I know you can, but it's heavy. I don't mind carrying it for a bit.'

She smiled at him. 'Right now you sound like my baby brother.'

'I guess,' he said, 'that's a step up from being like your ten-year-old.'

'Oh, you remind me of him as well,' she said, laughing.

Pippa wished she'd thought to ask Rory about the dress code. Did he wear a suit to do interviews, or would he opt for something more smart-casual? She'd chosen navy Capri pants, a navy top with stylised white daisies, flat shoes, and her hair was pulled back in a low ponytail, tied with a navy chiffon scarf. Hopefully it would be smart enough, but not over-formal.

When she came out of the Tube station, she looked round to find Rory. He was standing by the wall, a few paces away, with his camerawoman; clearly they had a good relationship, because they were laughing and Kenise was patting his shoulder. To her relief, he was wearing a white shirt, chinos and no tie: smart casual, then. Kenise was dressed all in black, which didn't surprise her; in her experience, photographers tended to wear black so they'd blend into the background and make their subjects relax, and she assumed that it was the same for video camerawork.

Today she'd get to see him at work, learn more about what made him tick—and she was really looking forward to it. Because they might be working together, she reminded herself; not because it meant a chance to spend more time with him.

Though she'd really enjoyed talking with him in the art gallery.

'Good morning,' she said brightly as she joined them.

'Ready to go? It's about a ten-minute walk,' Rory said.

Judith Parrish's flat was on the bottom floor of a Victorian house. Judith herself was a slight woman about the same height as Pippa, dressed in black trousers and a black T-shirt, her dark hair in a pixie cut.

'Lovely to meet you, Judith,' Rory said warmly, shaking her hand. 'This is Kenise, my camerawoman; and Pippa Barnes, the ballet dancer from the Fitzroy we spoke about yesterday.'

'Lovely to meet you, all,' Judith said. 'Come in.'

She ushered them into a living room which had gorgeous parquet flooring and a rug in the centre; an upright piano was set against one wall, with a cello case next to it; there was a sofa under the window, two tub chairs and a coffee table, and bookshelves in the alcove either side of the fireplace, which looked full of music scores.

'Would you mind if we moved the furniture a little?' Kenise asked. 'I'd like you and Rory to sit opposite each other in the tub chairs for the interview, but I could do with some room to move round you for extra shots.'

'Help yourself,' Judith said. 'Though I'd prefer the piano and cello to stay where they are.'

'Of course,' Rory said.

Judith smiled. 'I'll make some coffee.'

'Can I do anything to help?' Pippa asked.

'It's fine,' Judith said. Once she'd checked how everyone took their drinks, she headed for the kitchen while Rory and Kenise checked lighting and moved the chairs where they wanted them; Pippa sat on the sofa, out of the way.

When Judith came back and the drinks had been handed round, Rory said to her, 'I do have a list of questions, but basically we're going to chat and Kenise is going to film our conversation. I might stop you and ask you to repeat something, or ask you something in a different way—it doesn't mean you've done anything wrong, just that I'm keeping my options open when I come to edit the piece. Anything you don't want to answer, that's fine, and we can edit the question out without making it look awkward. If you can include my question in your answer, that'd be helpful, but it doesn't matter if you forget.'

Pippa listened, fascinated, as he got Judith to talk about her experience with music and how she developed a score.

Discovering that Judith had gone to a costumed Regency ball in Bath fanned the flames of the idea she'd had the previous day about creating something new for Rory's series.

Clearly he'd thought about it again, too, because he asked, 'The way Judith develops a score: is that how you develop choreography, Pippa?'

'It's a very similar process,' Pippa said. 'Just as Judith watches a film and works out the mood and the music to suit, I listen to music and work out the phrasing and which movements fit.'

'How long would it take to compose a two-minute piece and choreograph it?' Rory asked.

'Working out the choreography and writing it down might take an hour, maybe two,' Pippa said. 'Then I need to learn it so it's automatic, in my muscle memory. If I'm teaching someone else, I'd break it down into smaller phrases, and keep repeating them until the dancers know them.' She smiled. 'As you'll find out when you learn the dances for your series.'

'I could write something fairly quickly,' Judith said. 'I'd talk to the choreographer about the themes and the story we want to tell, and between us we'd come up with ideas we could work up. So if you wanted something set on a frosty winter night, say, I'd come up with staccato, glittery phrases.' She grinned. 'I'm cheating massively here because obviously this isn't mine, but winter, for me...' She walked over to the piano, sat down, and played the beginning of the 'Dance of the Sugar Plum Fairy'.

'You need quick, light movements in the choreography to match that,' Pippa said. She looked at the centre of room then at Judith. 'Would it be all right if I roll the rug back, take off my shoes and show him?'

'Of course,' Judith said.

'You don't necessarily need ballet shoes to dance. Obviously I don't have my pointe shoes with me so I'll do everything on demi—that's tiptoes, to you,' she said to Rory with a smile. 'Judith, please could you play something wintry?'

'How about this?' Judith played the middle section of the first movement of Vivaldi's 'Winter' from *Four Seasons*.

'Perfect—give me a minute or two to warm up,' Pippa said.

'I'll play from the start and you come in when you're ready?' Judith suggested.

Pippa did a very quick warm-up, then executed some light, quick but graceful movements when Judith got to the middle section. She finished with a pose and smiled at Rory. 'See? A frosty morning.'

'You just did that off the top of your head?' Rory asked.

'No. It's the "Fred Step"—the signature piece of the choreographer Frederick Ashton,' Pippa explained. 'It's a series of steps and you can repeat them however you like.'

'In a lot of music there's a short phrase which is repeated, inverted, then repeated again,' Judith said. She turned to Rory. 'What's your series about?

Rory explained it to her. 'Though I'm beginning to think it'd be good to ask the dancers to develop a new piece, too—say, two or three minutes.' He looked at Judith. 'Would you consider composing something for me?'

'I'd be happy to talk to your choreographers,' Judith said. She looked at Pippa. 'If that includes you, would you be happy to work with me on a piece?'

'I haven't actually agreed to do the series,

yet,' Pippa said, 'but I'm leaning that way—and I love the idea of doing something fresh. Maybe you could include a bit about choreography for all of them, Rory,' she suggested.

'We could maybe do something wintry,' Judith said thoughtfully.

'Or maybe a year in a garden: spring with everything growing, summer all lush and in bloom, autumn with leaves coming down, and a frosty winter morning,' Pippa suggested.

'With you wearing a glittery tutu?' Judith asked.

'Or a chiffon skirt, one colour for each season,' Pippa said. 'At the end of each "movement" I could go offstage, where Wardrobe would be waiting to swap my skirt.'

'While you're changing costume, we'd have a short musical transition between the seasons,' Judith said.

'I wish we'd been recording that,' Rory said ruefully. 'It would've been perfect to include in the dance series.'

'Actually, I did record it,' Kenise said. 'Including Pippa dancing. I just need some noddies from you now, Rory.'

'What are noddies?' Pippa asked.

'Shots of Rory nodding his head with his listening face on—we use them in editing. You'll see it in TV interviews all the time,' Kenise explained.

She'd need to learn new jargon, then; though Rory would also need to learn new things. The more Pippa thought about it, the more she was tempted to do his show. And, if she was honest with herself, the more she was tempted by Rory himself...

Later that day, Rory took Pippa to the TV offices to review the footage from the interview. He showed her what he would cut, where he was going to splice in a section of an old home video Judith had sent, and where the film trailer with Judith's music would fit in.

'It's like putting together a gala show—making sure you balance each section and mix up the tender and the dramatic pieces, the solos and the ensembles,' Pippa said. 'And I get why Kenise filmed your noddies.'

'I ought to let you get back,' he said.

She smiled. 'I'd appreciate a reminder on how to get to the front door. All those corridors look the same.'

'I'll walk you out,' he said. 'I need to give your visitor's pass back, too.' He paused. 'What do I need to wear for the conditioning class tomorrow?'

'Whatever you'd normally wear to the gym,' she said. 'If you've got close-fitting tracksuit bottoms, that'd be good. And bring water.'

'Got it,' he said. 'Thank you for coming with me to see Judith today. And for your ideas—I never thought about getting everyone to do new choreography to original music.'

'I think it'd give the show an edge,' she said. 'But it's your show—and your call.'

'It's a collaboration,' he said, 'because we all have to work as a team for it to come together.'

'I guess,' she said.

She handed her badge in at the reception area and was signed out.

Rory walked outside with her. 'See you tomorrow.' He leaned forward as if to kiss her on the cheek. Except somehow his lips connected with the corner of her mouth.

'Sorry,' he mumbled.

Pippa's face felt hot, and she didn't dare look him in the eye. 'It's OK.'

'I…um…' His voice faded, as if he didn't know what to say.

'See you tomorrow,' she said, and headed in the direction of the Tube station. She could still feel the touch of his lips at the corner of her mouth, and it sent a shiver of pure desire through her. Far from being a friendly peck on the cheek, it had turned into something else entirely.

She was going to have to be very, very careful…

Rory headed for the Fitzroy Theatre on Tuesday morning, really hoping that he hadn't messed everything up yesterday. How could he have been so clumsy? He'd felt so at ease with Pippa that it had been natural to kiss her cheek—except he hadn't.

He'd kissed the corner of her mouth.

And although he'd apologised immediately and she'd said everything was fine, he knew it wasn't. She'd really blushed. Luckily she hadn't returned his gaze, because his face had felt as hot as hers had looked.

The worst thing was, he hadn't been able to stop thinking about it since. Being that close to her. What would it be like to kiss her properly? What would it be like if she kissed him back?

Had her blush been purely from embarrassment, or had she felt the same spark of desire that he had? Had she been thinking about their kiss, too, and wondering what it would be like if they really connected?

Even the thought of it made his mouth tingle with need.

He was going to have to be really careful

today. Act all cool and calm and collected, even though inside he wasn't. He could focus on work…couldn't he?

Just as he walked up the steps, Pippa was there.

'Good morning. Ready for class?'

'Yes,' he fibbed. She was acting all brisk and breezy and professional, as if nothing had happened yesterday, so he'd follow her lead.

'Good. We're going through the stage door,' she said, shepherding him round to the back of the building and letting him in through an unobtrusive entrance. 'Here's the changing area, and this is the key for one of the guest lockers,' she said, giving him a key with a number on the fob. 'I'll meet you back here in five minutes and take you through to Kenzo's class.'

He changed in record time, put his things in the numbered locker and was ready when she came back to collect him.

The room she took him to was similar to his gym, with mirrors on one long side. The only difference was that there were barres fixed to three of the walls.

A man who looked to be in his mid-thirties, with an incredibly athletic physique, was setting out hand weights and resistance bands. He looked up as they walked in. 'Morning, Pippa,' he said.

'Morning, Kenzo.' She smiled at him. 'Rory, this is Kenzo, our physical development lead,' she said. 'Kenzo, this is Rory. He's making a programme about ballet—Nathalie's spoken to you about it.'

He nodded. 'It's a good idea to come and do a class so you get an insight into what it takes to be a dancer, Rory. Do you have any gym experience?'

'I do weights twice a week,' Rory said. 'I used to enjoy walking but that'll have to be strictly outside wasp season for me now; I'm planning to go to the gym for cardio instead.'

'Sensible,' Kenzo said. 'I'll just check anyway—you know how to engage your core?'

Rory nodded.

'Good. Any injuries or health conditions I need to know about—apart from the wasp allergy, obviously?'

'No, and I've got my adrenaline pens with me,' Rory said.

'Glad to hear it,' Kenzo said. 'You'll probably know some of the exercises we do, but some might feel a little bit different because you'll use a dancer's position. Have you done glute bridges and calf raises before?'

'Yes,' Rory said.

'Good. It's all about strength and flexibility,' Kenzo said. 'The ones you probably won't know—Pippa, can you demonstrate plié squats?'

'Sure,' she said. 'This is second position feet.' She stood with her feet apart, her toes turned out to the sides. 'Then you need second position arms.' She talked him through it. 'Start with bas bras—that's lowered arms—lift them up to first, as if you're holding a beach ball, then stretch your arms out to second, keeping them curved. Don't let your elbows drop.'

Realising she was expecting him to copy her moves, Rory did so. He looked down at his feet. 'I can't get my feet to go out the way yours are.'

'I wouldn't expect it,' Kenzo said. 'Work within the limits of what's comfortable for you, and do the turnout as far as you can.'

'Then you do the plié—bend your knees as you lower your body until your thighs are parallel with the floor. Back straight, chest lifted.' Pippa looked at him critically as he copied her. '*Nearly*. Can I move your arms?'

'Sure,' he said, hoping he sounded much more cool, calm and collected than he actually felt. Even though it was an impersonal contact, his skin still tingled where she touched him to move his arms into the right position. What would it be like to feel her fingertips skating across his skin if they were alone, in a private space?

'Then push through your heels and straighten your legs,' she said. 'That's good.'

Next, she demonstrated arabesque lifts.

'There's no *way* my leg's going to go up that far behind me,' Rory said ruefully.

'Not the first time, but gradually your flexibility will improve. Do this every day for a month—you'll really see the difference in your movements,' Kenzo said.

'The same as with a relevé—a rise,' Pippa said. 'Face the wall and use the barre to get your balance—you can do this with the back of a chair at home. Feet together in parallel, then rise onto the balls of your feet.'

He followed her instructions.

'When you're ready, lift your hand from the barre and balance,' she said.

He lasted for three seconds before he started wobbling.

She smiled, but she wasn't laughing at him or pitying him. It was more like fellow feeling—encouragement, and it made him feel warm inside.

'Do that four or five times every day,' she said, 'and I guarantee you'll be able to hold the position for ages and move both arms into a variety of positions without your feet wobbling by the end of the month.'

'It's really good for balance and stability,' Kenzo said.

The final movement Pippa showed him was a port de bras, involving light hand weights and moving his arms in a similar way to the first exercise, plus lifting them over his head in what he always thought of as the 'classic' ballerina arms.

'Try to lift from your back, not your shoulders,' Kenzo said. 'Stand at the barre next to Pippa; you can follow her if you need to because she knows the routine. And we can have a chat after the class. Pippa said you wanted to know the science behind the training. I can show you what we do here, and you can let me know what you'd want to film—or what you'd want to try.'

'Thank you,' Rory said. 'That's really helpful.'

The rest of the class filed in. All the female dancers were wearing leotards and leggings with a cardigan, while the male dancers wore form-fitting tracksuit bottoms, shirts and hoodies.

'Everyone, this is Rory,' Pippa said. 'He presents an arts show on TV. He's joining us for today's class with Kenzo, then observing rehearsals and class with Nathalie's agreement.'

'Are you the one whose life Pippa saved at the garden party?' one of the other dancers asked.

'Yes, and I'm very grateful,' Rory said.

Kenzo started music for the warm up, then gave instructions for the moves. Thanks to the quick introduction Pippa had given him, Rory didn't feel completely useless.

His chat with Kenzo afterwards meant that he missed seeing Pippa's class, but he was able to watch the first set of rehearsals. He stayed for lunch—she'd brought an extra wrap for him—then watched the full rehearsal in the afternoon. It was a dress rehearsal for *Swan Lake*, and Pippa was dancing the role of Odile/ Odette. He'd seen the ballet several times, over the years, but Pippa's performance really stood out for him. Not just the perfection of the technical stuff, which was impressive in its own right, but the way she made him *feel* the story. He could really believe she'd been enchanted and turned into a swan, and only the love of the handsome Prince could break the spell. It had made him want to rush onto the stage, hold her close, and tell her that he'd fight the wicked sorcerer for her.

Which would be the worst thing he could do, and it would make her run a mile.

Why was he even letting himself think about her in those terms?

He really needed to get a grip.

'I don't know what they're called,' he said

when she walked off the stage and joined him in the auditorium, 'but that bit when you're Odile and you do all those pirouettes at the end—that was absolutely amazing.'

'The famous thirty-two fouettés,' she said. 'That piece is notorious, technically, because you're supposed to stay in one place and it's very easy to travel a little bit.'

'You looked to me as if you stayed in one place. But how did you not get dizzy?' he asked.

'Spotting,' she said. 'You look at one place in the room and watch it for as long as you can before you turn your head, and bring your head back as quickly as possible.'

'I'd better let you rest before tonight's show,' he said, 'but thank you for arranging today with Nathalie and Kenzo.'

'You're very welcome,' she said. 'Are you coming to do the class tomorrow?'

'If you don't mind,' he said, 'and maybe I can watch your class afterwards, as I missed it today?'

'No problem,' she said.

He collected his things from the locker, and she walked out through the foyer with him.

'I hope the show goes—' he began.

'"Break a leg" is what you say,' she cut in swiftly. 'Dancers are a superstitious lot, and that includes me.'

'Break a leg,' he said.

Not wanting to make the same mistake he'd made the previous evening, he contented himself with shaking her hand. His fingers tingled where his skin touched hers. He was going to have to learn to deal with this, and fast, because he didn't want to put her off doing the show with him.

Though it wasn't the only reason he needed to keep himself at a distance. She'd made it clear that she wanted her involvement with him to remain on a purely professional level.

'See you for breakfast tomorrow in the café round the corner?' he asked.

'Ten past eight at the latest,' she said. 'We need enough time to digest breakfast before class.'

'All right. Ten past eight,' he said.

Though he couldn't stop thinking about her all the way home. That evening, when he was doing some research, he found himself doodling her name in the margins of his notes. It felt horribly like being a teenager all over again, and he was beginning to see what she meant about him distracting her; she was certainly distracting him. Even though he knew there was no sense to it, he *wanted* her. And it wasn't going to happen.

'For pity's sake, Rory, stop whining and get

on with your work,' he told himself loudly, and tried to focus on the book he'd picked up from the library.

It didn't work.

A cold shower didn't help, either.

All he could think about was her. Seizing the day. Making the most of every minute.

In the end, he made himself a mug of tea and thought about it. There was definitely something between them; her reaction when he'd accidentally kissed the corner of her mouth told him that she felt the same kind of pull.

She didn't want a relationship.

He didn't want a relationship.

So was there a compromise? Could they, perhaps, have a mad fling? Knowing that there wasn't the pressure of a future and anyone else's expectations, maybe they could simply enjoy their physical reaction to each other. No strings, no pressure, no distraction: just mutual pleasure.

He'd have to work out a way of asking her without making it sound demanding or sleazy.

But maybe if they could get it out of both their systems, they'd be able to concentrate.

On Wednesday morning, Rory walked into the café at five past eight. He thought he might beat her to it, but Pippa was already there, sitting at a table with a coffee. She waved to him and smiled, and his heart felt as if it had done a backflip.

'Morning. I haven't ordered food yet, but I needed a coffee,' she said as he slid into the seat opposite her.

'What do you recommend?' he asked.

'Everything's good, here—but I'm having scrambled eggs on seeded toast,' she said. 'And then Greek yogurt with blueberries and chia seeds.'

'Scrambled eggs sounds good,' he said. 'Though I could be tempted by a blueberry muffin.'

Once the waitress had taken their order, she asked, 'How do you feel, this morning?'

Better for seeing her. Not that he could tell her that. 'A tiny bit stiff,' he admitted.

'You need to do some stretching in the evening if your muscles are tight. Stretching's the thing that everyone forgets in the gym because they're in a rush,' she said.

'I'm definitely guilty of that,' he said. 'I know I need to warm up before a workout, but I'm not always good at remembering to cool down afterwards.'

'It only takes five minutes, and it'll make a difference,' she said. 'So what's your schedule looking like, this week?'

'Research for the dance show, talking to some experts, seeing a curator about an exhibition of commonplace books, and I've got an interview tomorrow morning with a stained-glass restorer working on some of the oldest stained-glass in England,' he said. 'I'm going to Norfolk for that one.'

'Sounds interesting,' she said.

'I'd offer to let you come with me,' he said, 'but I assume you're working?'

'I am,' she said, 'though I'm not dancing tomorrow night. If you're free tomorrow evening and you're back from Norfolk, you could come and watch the show in the wings with me.'

'I'd like that very much,' he said.

When they did Kenzo's class, he was aware that everyone else was much more graceful than he was, and had a much wider range of movements; but he could also balance a little more easily than he had, the previous day.

On Thursday, he found he actually missed doing the conditioning class. But the interview went well, and when he met Pippa at the Fitzroy that evening he thoroughly enjoyed watching *Swan Lake* from a very privileged position in the wings, seeing how things worked backstage. He remembered what she'd told him about how slickly the wardrobe, make-up and hair team worked, and he could see it in action for himself.

And, best of all, Pippa reached for his hand when Odile was pretending to be Odette and seducing Siegfried into marrying him. She kept holding his hand during the whole of the last act, when Siegfried realised his mistake and tried to find Odette. He realised she was crying, and moved closer to her, releasing her hand and sliding his arm round her shoulders to comfort her; and he was surprised to realise that his own lashes were wet, too.

'Sorry about that,' Pippa said at the end of the curtain calls, mopping her eyes with a tissue and moving slightly so Rory dropped his arm from round her shoulders. 'Though I did warn you that *Swan Lake* makes me cry, every single time.'

'It's very emotional,' he agreed. 'The music, the dance, all together…it's quite a spectacle.'

They walked back to the Tube station together; his hand brushed against hers once, twice, making little sparks rush through her. And then his fingers caught hers lightly.

Maybe it was the emotion left over from the show, and remembering how good it had felt to have his arm round her, holding her close through the final dramatic act, but she didn't pull her hand away.

And they were still loosely holding hands when they got to the station.

She wasn't ready to let go.

His expression told her it was the same for him.

Common sense. That was what she needed. A neutral conversation. Small talk. Don't look at his lips or start to wonder how they'd feel. He'd made it clear he wasn't looking for a relationship. She wasn't, either.

So why couldn't she untangle her fingers from his? Why couldn't she stop looking at his mouth?

'Did you enjoy the view from the wings?' she asked—and hoped he didn't hear the rustiness in her voice.

'Stunning,' he said. 'You were right about the magic of the performance—even when you know how things work, it doesn't stop you enjoying the spectacle.'

'I love watching from the wings. You can feel the buzz from the audience as well as the energy from the stage,' she said.

'I think I get that, now,' he said.

He was definitely looking at her mouth, before glancing up at her eyes.

And she knew she was doing the same. Wondering. Thinking about it.

She wasn't sure which of the two of them moved first, but then her arms were round his neck and his were round her waist, and they were kissing. Tiny, tentative brushes of their lips against each other, teasing and tempting, building the heat, until she felt as if she were burning up from the inside.

She broke the kiss, but she couldn't take her arms from round his neck.

'That wasn't supposed to happen,' he said, and she was gratified to hear that he sounded as shaken as she felt.

'We shouldn't be doing this,' she said, trying to talk herself into moving away from him, even while she yearned to be closer.

Except he was clearly listening to the words she was saying and didn't realise how much he tempted her, because he said, 'You're right, it's a bad idea,' and disentangled himself gently from her.

Hearing him agree with her common sense so easily and so rapidly made her wish that he'd raised at least a token protest. How stupid she'd been, virtually throwing herself at him.

Her misery must have shown on her face, because he said quietly, 'I admit—I wanted to kiss you, and half of me doesn't regret doing it.'

Which meant that half of him *did* regret it. So he was as torn as she was, between the common sense that said 'don't take the risk', and the longing that said 'forget the world and do it now'.

He stroked her face. 'We can't get involved with each other. Even if we—' his voice cracked slightly '—want to. You're focused on your career. I'm focused on my documentary, and hoping it opens doors for my future. Neither of us has the space in our lives for any kind of relationship.'

He was talking complete sense.

But.

Was it her imagination, or did his eyes hold a very different message? He'd said half of him *didn't* regret it. That he'd wanted to kiss her, too.

'And I want you to be in my documentary. I don't want to ruin our working relationship,' he finished.

'I don't want to ruin that, either,' she said. 'I don't want to get distracted and lose my promotion. Or to have to choose between ballet and a relationship, because I can't give enough to both of them at the same time.'

'I've given up dating. I've been there, done that, made all the wrong choices,' he said. And then he moistened his lower lip. 'But.'

Oh, God. She wanted to kiss him again. Right here, right now, until they were both dizzy. Suddenly it was hard to breathe. 'But?'

'This *thing*—this pull between us…it's not just me, is it?' he checked.

The vulnerability in his expression made her tell the truth. 'No.'

'I could walk away from you now,' he said. 'Put you back at arm's length. Except I know how much I'd regret it.'

So would she. Because she'd never felt this kind of attraction to anyone else. She'd always been too focused on her job to even *notice* anyone else.

'What are you suggesting?' she asked.

'Maybe,' he said, 'we need to do the crazy thing. Get it out of our systems. And then, once we've done that, we can go back to being sensible.'

'You think that would work?' Because she wasn't convinced that a fling would actually get him out of her system. 'What if we…?'

'Fall in love? We won't,' he said. 'Neither of us want a relationship. Both of us want to chase our dreams. So that makes a fling safe for us. We're on the same page. No strings, no promises, no holding each other back. And because we know it's temporary, right from the start, neither of us will get hurt. Neither of us will be let down. Neither of us will get distracted from our dreams.'

'Uh-huh.' It sounded perfect. But what if…?

Clearly her doubts showed, because he sighed. 'If I'm being honest, I'm not entirely sure it'll work. But right now we're both distracted anyway. We might as well be distracted and enjoy it, than distracted and…well…' He groaned. 'See, that's proof. Before I met you, I was never incoherent. But, the first time I met you, I made next to no sense when I spoke.'

'To be fair, you'd just been stung by a wasp and were having a massive anaphylactic reaction,' she said.

He nodded. 'That's the thing. Nearly dying has made me realise how precious life is—how I should make the most of every minute. That's why I don't want to walk away from you—from whatever this is.'

She raised her eyebrows at him. 'You sound like a seventeenth-century poet telling me to seize the day.'

He raised his eyebrows back at her. 'You did A level sciences. I didn't think you'd know Herrick and Marvell.'

'Some of my fellow dancers did English—and they love sharing poetry,' she said. '"Gather ye rosebuds while ye may."'

'As long as there aren't any wasps in the roses,' he said wryly.

'So what do we do now?' she asked.

'I want you, Pippa,' he said simply. 'I know

you're busy at work. I know you're driven and you want that promotion more than anything else. I respect that, and I'm not looking to change you. I want you to do my show, because I love the way you dance and I think you'd be fabulous on screen. I think my viewers are going to fall in love with you. If you want to keep things between us strictly work, that's fine. We'll both be sensible and do that. But if you want to be with me, too—keeping everything low key, no pressure, no demands—that's also fine.' His eyes held hers. 'It's your choice.'

She could keep herself strictly focused on her work; or she could give in to the attraction and see what happened. He had the same reservations that she did; and he was right. They were on the same page. This would be safe.

'You're busy at work, too,' she said. 'Your documentary series could lead to all sorts of things—maybe opportunities to work abroad. Paris, America, Australia. And I'm based here. It'd be sensible to…well, not start something we can't finish.'

'I know. But I don't want to be sensible,' he said. 'I want to make the most of every second.'

And maybe they could do that without making promises. Or *almost* no promises. 'It's exclusive, while it lasts?'

'Neither of us has the time for a fling with

each other, let alone a fling with someone else as well.' He brushed the pad of his thumb against her lower lip. 'But, yes, it would be exclusive.'

'All right,' she said. 'I'll do the show.' She paused. 'And…'

'And?' he asked, his voice rough with need.

'Carpe diem,' she said, and kissed him.

CHAPTER EIGHT

On Friday, Rory was busy at the studio all day but couldn't stop thinking about Pippa. He still couldn't quite believe that he'd asked her to have a fling with him—or that she'd agreed to it. He went hot all over at the memory of the way she'd kissed him last night. How long had it been since someone had made him feel like a teenager?

But he managed to focus on his guests for the show, and made sure they all enjoyed the experience. Showbiz was a small world, and he wanted to keep his reputation of being a pleasure to work with rather than risk people thinking that he was just dialling it in.

Later that evening, his phone pinged with a text from Pippa.

Loved the show. Want to have breakfast tomorrow?

He knew she was due at the Fitzroy at nine-fifteen sharp for Kenzo's class. He texted back.

Our café, five past eight?

Works for me. Come to class after?

Sure. How did Swan Lake go tonight?

Fine. Thirty minutes of curtain calls!

Deserved, he thought. Watching her dance was a joy.

When he woke, the next morning, even though it was raining it felt like a beautiful day—because he was going to be seeing Pippa.

He was sitting in the café at eight o'clock, literally a minute before she walked through the door. How beautiful she was, he thought, how graceful and lovely; she made the day feel brighter just by walking into a room.

'Hey,' she said and sat opposite him.

'Hey, you,' he said, smiling back. 'I missed not seeing you yesterday.'

'I missed not seeing you, too,' she admitted.

When the waitress came over, she ordered coffee and eggs Florentine; he ordered the same.

'What are you dancing tonight?' he asked.

'One of the Two Swans,' she said.

'You look so cute in a tutu,' he said.

She dipped her head in acknowledgement. 'Thank you.'

'Cute, full stop,' he added.

Her grin widened. 'I know someone very cute, too. Though I don't think I'd put him in a tutu.'

'How would you dress me for ballet?' he asked, suddenly curious.

'As the Stranger, in Matthew Bourne's *Swan Lake*. All in black. That dance in Act Three is *incredibly* sexy. Or Oberon in *The Dream*, with a spiky crown and fairy wings and an outfit that looks as if you're part of the forest, wreathed in ivy and berries.' She took her phone out and found him a photograph. 'Like this. All wild and elemental.'

He looked at the photo. 'Very Green Man.' And not at all how he saw himself.

'As a character, I think Oberon needs his comeuppance. But he's very pretty to look at,' she said.

'I'll take that as a compliment,' he said. 'For the record, I agree with you. I don't know the ballet, but I know the play—and Oberon is an arse. In his shoes, I wouldn't have tried to steal the child from Titania or tried to humiliate her.'

'I know.' She blew him a kiss, and he went hot all over.

To the point where he just blurted it out. 'I was thinking—as tomorrow's Sunday, you don't have to be at the Fitzroy in the morning. Can I make you dinner tonight after the show?'

'That's very kind of you to offer,' she said.

Wanting to circumvent the 'but' that he could see so obviously in her face, he said, 'I can drive you home from my place after dinner.' He paused. 'Or—if you want to—you could stay over. I have a spare toothbrush. Maybe we can do something tomorrow, if you're free.'

'Sorry. I'm going to see my sisters tomorrow,' she said.

They'd only agreed on their fling last night. It was just between the two of them. It was ridiculous—more than that, it was unreasonable, he told himself sharply—to feel disappointed that she didn't want to introduce him to her family. 'Have fun,' he said.

'My sisters think I'm a horrible workaholic who needs a social life. If they met you, they'd drive me crackers with a ton of questions.'

'To be fair, you *are* a workaholic who needs a social life,' he said. 'But I rather like being a workaholic, too. And I don't want a social life like the one I had a few months ago.'

'Are you saying it takes one to know one?' she teased, her gorgeous eyes crinkling at the corners.

'Yes. So can I cook you dinner tonight?' he asked.

'I'd like that—and you're welcome to come and watch the show in the wings, if you're not busy,' she said.

He was, but he'd catch up with work later. 'I'd love that,' he said.

'Come to the stage door for quarter to seven,' she said, 'and I'll take you through.'

After breakfast, they did the conditioning class. This time round, Rory found it easier.

Kenzo came over to him at the end of the class. 'Well done. I can see the improvement in your balance already.'

'Thank you,' Rory said, feeling as if he'd achieved something.

'Told you so,' Pippa said with a cheeky wink. 'See you later.'

Later. When he needed to impress her with his cooking—no, he corrected mentally, he needed to be *himself*. This wasn't about him. She'd be hungry after the performance and wouldn't want to wait hours for him to fuss about in the kitchen. He could cheat and buy something from the chiller section at the supermarket, but he wanted to make a bit more of an effort. Something that he could make this morning, leave in the fridge, and reheat quickly tonight. For pudding, he played it safe, buying a selection of summer berries and a tub of really good vanilla ice cream.

Back in his kitchen, he roasted chunks of aubergine on a tray with tomatoes and garlic, and made a batch of gnocchi. Once the vegetables were done, he finished making the Norma sauce; the flavours would develop nicely in the fridge during the day, and when he and Pippa got back here after the show it would take about five minutes to boil the kettle, cook the gnocchi and reheat the sauce.

Satisfied that dinner would be fine, he spent the afternoon researching for his documentary and making notes.

After the final close of the curtain, Pippa showered and changed, then met Rory in the auditorium.

'I've called a taxi,' he said, 'because it's quicker at this time of night. We'll be home in ten minutes.'

She knew Notting Hill was pretty, but she couldn't help being charmed when the taxi dropped them on one of the cobbled streets. The mews houses in Rory's street were all painted pretty pastel ice-cream colours; his house was cream, and there were bay trees in terracotta pots either side of the grey front door. Other houses had pots of tulips underneath the window; one had an old tin bath full of herbs; and one had a beautiful canopy of wisteria.

'What a gorgeous neighbourhood,' she said.

'Thank you.' He smiled at her. 'I love it, here—and I'm lucky because all my neighbours are nice, too.' He unlocked the front door and ushered her inside. 'The bathroom's here on the left,' he said gesturing to a door; the other side of the hallway appeared to be cupboards.

Inside, the entire ground floor had been opened up into one room, with a stripped pale wooden floor and cream walls. There was a pale grey kitchen in an alcove at one end of the room. The dining area was in the middle of the room, next to a cast-iron fireplace; the table was already set for two. At the far end was a comfortable living room area with a large sofa, bookshelves and a state-of-the-art TV.

There were exquisite framed paintings on the walls, and an open staircase leading up to the next floor. One of the paintings looked familiar. 'Isn't that the picture you showed me in the National?' Pippa asked.

'It's a good-quality print,' he said. 'Though the oils are all originals. When I was interviewing the curator of the Hammershøi exhibition, she told me about a group of modern painters who were influenced by him. I went to their studios and bought the ones that caught my eye.'

'I'm sure I've heard someone say that when it comes to art it's better to buy something you love, rather than something you think will turn out to be an investment,' she said.

'That's a good rule,' he agreed.

'They're lovely. It's all about the light, isn't it?'

He nodded. 'Dinner will be literally five minutes. Can I get you a glass of wine?'

'Thank you for the offer, but it'd send me straight to sleep,' she said. 'Some water would be lovely, though, please.'

He went over to the kitchen area and fetched her a glass.

'Thank you. Is there anything I can do to help?' she asked.

'It's just a question of boiling the kettle for the gnocchi and heating the sauce through,' he said. 'Please, make yourself at home.' He lit the candle in the middle of the dining table and headed back to the kitchen area.

Pippa browsed the books on his shelves, glass in hand. As she'd expected, knowing that his degree was in English, there was lots of classic literature, plus a shelf of art books. The mantelpiece was covered with framed family photographs, very similar to her own collection: weddings, christenings, his graduation and what she assumed were the latest photographs of his nieces and nephews. Rory was clearly very close to his family.

He'd switched on a smart speaker, and a gentle Einaudi piece flooded into the room. It was the perfect music to chill to, she thought.

'Dinner is served, madam,' he said, a couple of minutes later, placing two bowls on the table. He turned the overhead light down so the candlelight flickered.

'This smells delicious,' she said as she sat opposite him.

'And it's properly home-made, not shop bought,' he said. 'Gnocchi with sauce *alla* Norma.'

She blinked. 'You made your own gnocchi?'

'It's pretty simple,' he said. 'And quick.'

'I appreciate it,' she said, and took a bite. 'Ooh, that's fabulous.'

'Thank you.' He looked pleased. 'Mum always said she didn't want to raise men who were domestically incompetent. She taught all of us to cook, and Jamie and I did just as many chores as Lottie when we were growing up.'

'But your dad's an earl. Surely you had...' She tried to think of a less inflammatory word than *servants*. 'People to help with the domestic stuff?'

'We do,' he said. 'The hall would be a bit much to handle without staff to help us, inside and out. But Mum wanted the three of us to have a normal-ish upbringing, so we'd grow up appreciating our privilege rather than becoming like those entitled twerps who treat people with contempt.'

'I like the sound of your mum,' Pippa said approvingly.

He smiled. 'Everyone gets on with my mum. She can be a bit bossy in a crisis, but that's probably a good thing—she doesn't panic or flap.' He wrinkled his nose. 'Apart from last week. That drove me bananas. Though, to be fair, the wasp thing gave her a bit of a scare.'

'It would have freaked everyone in my family, too, even though they're all doctors,' Pippa said. She looked at him. 'They all saw me on your show. And I felt there was a bit of "told you so" from them.'

'That you'd done the CPR well? To be fair, you did. You saved my life. And my family appreciate that, too.' He spread his hands. 'They also noticed the dancing and they're all getting tickets for the gala show.'

'I bought tickets for my family,' Pippa said.

He frowned. 'Surely they bought their own?' And then he must've remembered the little she'd told him, because he said, 'Or is that the only way you think they'll come to see you dance?'

'My sisters and brothers-in-law would. But my parents…it's awkward,' she said. 'Even giving them tickets felt as if I'm rubbing it in that I chose something they didn't want for me.'

'And when they do see you dance, you feel as

if you have to do twice as well as you've ever done before?' he asked gently. 'Pippa—you do *know* you dance like an angel?'

'Thank you but, I wasn't fishing for compliments,' she said.

'I know that,' he said. 'A career in the arts is hard enough, without the added pressure of feeling you've let people down by not doing what they wanted. Have you ever considered that they might be the ones letting *you* down, by not supporting you to follow your dreams?'

'Yes, but I'm the baby. I'm kind of meant to follow in their footsteps.' She sighed. 'I found a way to follow my dream. But that's why I have to get the promotion. Otherwise all the disappointment I've caused them, the way I've put dance as a priority over my family—that'd be for nothing.'

He reached across the table and squeezed her hands. 'You're good enough to get that promotion. And plenty of people prioritise their career, especially in the early years.'

'I don't do as much as I should to stay in touch,' she said. 'I feel guilty about that.'

'It goes both ways,' Rory said. 'If you're the one who always makes the phone calls, or always messages first—that's not fair.'

'They call me and message me,' Pippa said. 'But I don't make enough effort. I find excuses for why I can't drop in and see them. Usually work-related.'

'Once you've got the promotion, you'll have time to look at your work-life balance,' Rory said. 'But I get what you mean. My family try hard not to ask me if I've met someone or when I'm going to settle down—but that's more pressure than if they asked me straight out, because I can see what they're thinking. Whenever they ask me to some social event, I'm always wondering if they've invited someone to introduce me to.'

'Maybe you need to invent a partner,' she said.

'Maybe,' he said.

'But what I don't get,' she said. 'Is why you haven't already been snapped up?'

'Because I'm rubbish at picking dates,' he said. 'The last half a dozen—they've only wanted me because of who my family is, or because they think I can get them into celebrity parties, their photo in *Celebrity Life!* magazine, or I'd be a useful stepping stone in their own TV career. And I'm at the point where I think that being *myself* just isn't enough for anyone. I'm so tired of it. That's why I stopped dating.'

Not being enough.

She definitely knew how that felt.

Maybe she could help him; or maybe they

could help each other. 'Just to be clear: I don't want you for your family,' Pippa said. 'And me doing the documentary—that's a win for both of us.' She spread her hands. 'As for this thing… I'm see you exactly for who you are. Someone I like. Someone I find attractive. Someone who makes me see things in a slightly different way. So I guess in my eyes, you're enough just as you are.'

He took her hand, dropped a kiss on her palm and folded her fingers round it. 'That's a lovely thing to say.'

'I meant it,' she said.

His eyes were very, very blue. 'I appreciate it. Now, would you like coffee?'

Which was a very nice way of changing the subject, she thought. 'Not for me, thanks—though if you have any camomile tea, that'd be lovely.'

'Sorry.' He shook his head. 'Though my sister Lottie was on a health kick earlier this year and I bought green tea for her. Would that be OK?'

'No, it's fine. I'll stick with water,' she said. 'Can I do the washing up?'

'Absolutely not.' He looked at her. 'Would you like me to drive you home now? Or can I persuade you to stay a little longer and dance with me?'

Stay or go. He'd made it clear that it was her choice. They'd agreed: no strings, no pressure.

'What sort of dance?' she checked.

'A slow dance,' he said. 'Nothing formal or structured. Just you and me, and the kind of Saturday night radio station that plays all the old smoochy stuff without too much chatting in between.'

She couldn't remember the last time she'd done anything like that. 'That sounds good,' she said.

He switched the music to a digital radio station that was playing an old song she loved, Paul Weller's 'You Do Something to Me'; then he drew her into his arms. As they swayed softly together, he dipped his head so his cheek was right next to hers.

This wasn't the kind of dancing she did very often, but she loved the feeling of being so close to Rory: the soft music, the candlelight, the scent of the bergamot candles... When was the last time someone had done something this romantic with her? She had no idea, but right at that moment she felt *cherished*.

Giving in to temptation, she moved her head slightly, and the corners of their mouths touched.

And it was as if she'd just lit touchpaper, because all of a sudden they were kissing, really kissing, hot and urgent and needy.

When he broke the kiss, his pupils were huge in the candlelight, and she had no idea how long they'd been kissing. She just knew that her whole body was quivering with need.

'I can drive you home now,' he said. 'Or I can drive you home tomorrow morning, in time for you to meet your sisters.'

He'd really paid attention to what she'd said, she thought. And he wasn't demanding anything: he was giving her the choice.

'Tomorrow morning,' she said.

'I was hoping you'd say that,' he said. He kissed her again, scooped her up, blew out the candle, and carried her up the stairs.

CHAPTER NINE

THE NEXT MORNING, Pippa woke early; for a moment, the unfamiliar light in the room threw her, but then she remembered where she was. Rory was sprawled on the bed beside her; he looked very cute asleep. Sleeping Beauty, she thought, and she couldn't resist waking him with a kiss.

'Well, good morning,' he said, stroking her hair back from her face. 'And you've just made it that little bit better.'

Just as he'd promised, the previous night, he had a new toothbrush for her, and he'd put fresh towels in the bathroom, urging her to use whatever she wanted.

After a breakfast of toast and peanut butter, along with excellent coffee, he drove her back to Hackney. 'Have fun with your sisters,' he said.

'You have a lovely day, too,' she said.

'I'll spend it being nagged about wasps,' he said. 'Everyone's coming up to London for lunch with my parents.'

She leaned over to kiss him. 'I'm sure they

won't nag. They just want to see for themselves that you've recovered.'

'Maybe,' he said. 'At least I get the fun of playing cards with my nieces and nephews.' He laughed. 'Those angelic little faces hide the souls of pure card sharps.'

He looked the picture of a doting uncle as he talked about them, and a little warning bell rang in the back of her head. Did this mean Rory wanted children?

Not that it was a real issue. They were having a fling, which meant keeping it light and not serious. But maybe she needed to remember not to get carried away: not to get used to having him in her life, because she couldn't give him what he wanted and she didn't want to add him to the long, long list of people she'd already let down.

'That sounds familiar,' she said, forcing herself to smile brightly. 'With us it's Monopoly, and my youngest niece always seems to end up with all the green and purple sets. You should see the glee on her face when she collects the rent on multiple hotels.'

He chuckled, and kissed her back. 'Speak to you soon.'

The second he got to his parents' house he was wrapped in fierce hugs. Firstly by his mother, which he'd expected; secondly by his elder brother, which—given that Jamie really wasn't the demonstrative sort—he hadn't.

'I don't care if you're not the spare any more, since Phin was born—you're way more important to me than the estate is. You stay away from wasps, you hear?' Jamie asked, his eyes narrowing.

'Absolutely,' Lottie, his sister, agreed. 'And you need to wear this.'

Rory dubiously eyed the box she handed him. 'What is it?'

'Open it and put it on,' she said, putting her hands on her hips and fixing him with her bossiest stare.

He opened it to see a bracelet made from black plaited leather, with a silver tag embellished with a red medical alert symbol and engraved with the words *Anaphylaxis—info inside*.

'Wear it,' Lottie said. 'Then if anything happens and you can't get to your adrenaline pen in time, whoever comes to the rescue will see the bracelet and know to open this panel to get all your medical information.'

'It looks like a manacle,' he said.

'I don't care. It'll keep you safe.' Lottie added his third fierce hug of the morning. 'I don't want my baby brother at risk.'

'I won't be taking any risks,' he assured her.

'Just wear the bracelet,' Lottie said. 'Please. So I can sleep at night.'

He gave in and fastened it round his wrist. 'Happy, now?'

'Better,' Lottie said. 'But oh, dear God, when Mum rang us last weekend…'

'You rushed up to see me for yourself. You've spoken to me every day since, both of you. You know I'm absolutely fine,' Rory said. '*Really*. You two are the first people I'd come to if something was wrong, I promise. Just as I hope you know I'm there for you.'

She ruffled his hair. 'We do.'

Jamie gave him the gentlest punch. 'Yes. We do. But we still worry about you.'

'Don't,' Rory said. 'I might be the baby, but I'm sensible.'

'You're a TV star. Sensible and celeb don't go together,' Lottie teased.

He laughed. 'They do in my case.'

'Not when you keep dating unsuitable women,' she said. 'You need to find someone nice.'

He had—but he wasn't ready to talk about that, yet.

'Jamie and I could find you someone,' Lottie persisted.

'That's kind, but no. Consider me off the market. I'm concentrating on my career for now.'

As for Pippa… He liked her. A lot. But they'd agreed to nothing more serious than a fling. Looking to the future would put too much pressure on their relationship. No promises meant no disappointments—for both of them.

After lunch, the children all asked to go to the park.

'I'll stay here,' Rory said. 'The park's prime wasp territory. Much as I like playing football with you, I don't want to make it one-nil to the wasps.'

'We'll be on guard for you, Uncle Rory,' Phin, his oldest nephew, said immediately.

'We can flap at them so they fly away,' added seven-year-old Bertie, not to be outdone.

'Thanks for the offer, boys, but firstly you *never* flap at a wasp—it makes them panic and send out "help" signals, so the rest of their mates come to back them up. And, secondly, wasps can fly faster than you can run,' Rory said.

Phin scoffed. 'No *way*.'

'Yes, way,' Rory insisted. 'The average speed of a wasp is seven miles an hour.'

'But they wouldn't be able to fly very far,' Bertie said. 'They'd get tired and have to stop.'

'*Average* speed,' Rory said. 'If the wind's right, and it's really annoyed, a wasp can fly at speeds of up to thirty miles an hour.' He mimicked a wasp speeding over to them. 'Zzzzz…'

'Now you're really teasing us,' Phin said.

'Am I? As a journalist, I always do my research before I use facts and figures. Look it up, my young sceptic,' Rory said, handing over his phone.

Phin put the question into a search engine and narrowed his eyes as he read the answer. 'That's amazing!' he said at last.

'Wasps are amazing,' Rory said. 'Look up pictures of their nests. They're works of art— and it's incredible to think they're all made with wood-shavings and wasp spit.'

'Wasp spit? Yuck!' said Sarah, his oldest niece.

'It's clever stuff,' Rory said. 'Off to the park with you. I'm staying put. And, while you're out, I'll raid Granny's kitchen and make cake.'

'I want to make cakes with you, Uncle Rory! I don't want to play football,' Lydia, Lottie's three-year-old, said. 'We could make fairy cakes. Granny bought sparkles to go on the top.'

'OK to leave her with me, Lottie?' Rory asked.

'Just don't let her get completely covered in flour,' Lottie said, with a weary nod.

'We'll borrow one of Granny's tea towels and use it as an apron,' Rory said. 'And I like the sound of those sparkles. Come on, Lyds. Let's go and make cake.'

The rest of the adults headed off to the park with the children, leaving Rory with Lydia. He got his niece to count out the paper cases as she put them in the bun tin, helped her crack the eggs and fished out bits of shell when her back was turned, and helped her spoon the mixture into the cases. He thoroughly enjoyed making pink buttercream icing with her, letting her smear it all over the top of the fairy cakes; sprinkling tiny silver stars and pink edible glitter on top was huge fun.

By the time they'd finished baking—and Rory had managed to clear up the glitter, which had spread over a surprisingly large area of his mother's kitchen—all felt right again with his world. He was in the middle of a family he loved dearly, and who loved him all the way back. Though, weirdly, a little part of him was starting to wonder if his siblings were right. If he needed to start dating someone who'd fit in with their family, just by being herself. As for Pippa… Well, she had her own pressures to deal with. She didn't need to deal with his issues, too. He liked her. And that would have to be enough for now.

Later that evening, Pippa texted him.

Good day?

He typed back.

Excellent. You?

Pretty good. Want to come here for breakfast tomorrow?

Love to. Though I have an interview at ten.

She called him. 'Where's the interview?'

'The TV studios,' he said. 'King's Cross.'

'King's Cross is…let me check… Maybe forty-five minutes from here. Say you left here at nine. We'd still have time to have breakfast together.'

'I'll be there at eight,' he said. 'Anything you want me to bring?'

'Just you,' she said, and he could hear the smile in her voice.

All the same, the next morning, he took her something special in a sealed plastic tub.

'Made yesterday afternoon by Lydia, my youngest niece, and me, while the rest of them went to the park,' he said.

She opened the tub and smiled. 'How fabulous! I've never seen so much glitter on a fairy cake before. I'll save it for my afternoon snack. Please say thank you to her for me.'

'I will,' he promised.

'Though you took a risk, bringing that here, with all that sugar,' she said.

'No, I didn't. It was in a sealed tub. I assure you that not a single wasp twigged what I was carrying or tried to mug me for it,' he said. 'Besides, Lottie's making me wear a manacle. Look.' He held up his wrist in disgust. 'The joys of big sisters.'

'I have two,' she reminded him. 'Actually, a medical alert bracelet is quite a good idea.'

'It still looks like a manacle,' he grumbled.

'Never mind. You'll just have to tell everyone you're Spartacus,' she teased. 'The coffee's brewed. Come in and sit down.'

Her flat was a small one-bedroomed place on the first floor of a purpose-built modern block in Hackney. Like his house, it had wooden floors and cream-painted walls, though the art in her living room was all either floral or ballet-related. There was a framed print of Degas' dancers; another of a stylised tulip with a line drawing of a ballerina that turned the tulip into a skirt; a publicity poster for *The Nutcracker* from four years ago which he guessed had been one of her shows; and an amazing black and white photograph of a ballet dancer seeming to fly through the air while doing the splits…and then he realised that the ballerina was *her*.

'That's an amazing photo of you,' he said.

'Press photo from earlier this year,' she said. 'My sisters had it enlarged and framed for mc. They've each got one, too.'

She didn't mention her parents, he noticed, so he wouldn't mention them, either.

There were more framed photographs on a shelf, similar to his own collection—weddings, christenings, her sisters' graduation days, her nieces and nephews. The flowers he'd bought her earlier in the week were in a large vase on the coffee table, beautifully arranged. There was no TV, though. And no books.

She must've noticed him noticing, because she said, 'I tend to read eBooks rather than paperbacks; it's easier, because I read on the Tube or during my breaks at work.'

'I'm not judging you,' he said. 'I just have a lot of books from my student days. And a TV because—well, work.'

'I'm not judging you, either,' she said with a smile, and handed him the mug of coffee. 'Take a seat.'

The table was laid for two; she'd set out a jug of freshly squeezed orange juice, a bowl of berries and a tub of Greek yogurt. A couple of minutes later, she came to join him, carrying a basket of warmed brioche buns and a plate of bacon. 'Help yourself,' she said. 'Sorry, I don't have any ketchup.'

'That's fine. This is all lovely,' he said. 'I like your flat.'

'It's small,' she said, 'but it's home.' She slotted some bacon into a brioche bun. 'What's the subject of your interview, this morning?'

'It's for the dance series. I'm talking to a ballroom dance teacher,' he said. 'She won some pretty big competitions, in her professional days. Nowadays she teaches in community halls, and hosts professional tea dances—people can just turn up for a cup of tea, a slice of cake and a dance, and there's no bar on age or ability. She's talking to me this morning about the benefits of dance and ageing.'

'Co-ordination, balance, and keeping you mentally sharp because you have to think about the music and the movement, which in turn makes connections in your brain,' she said. 'I've read some good articles on that. Plus there's the social aspect. I have friends who teach classes for beginners or older adults, and there's always a coffee after class. I'm guessing her students usually go off somewhere for a drink and a chat afterwards.'

He nodded. 'She says she has a band with a singer for the tea dances, but she uses taped music for her classes. She's going to teach me for two hours a day, to fit in between her classes and my work.'

'Sounds good,' she said. 'I assume all your teachers are going to take you through the basic steps, then teach you a routine. Which ballroom dance are you doing?'

'She said she wanted to teach me something new, so not the waltz—she says the quickstep's fun. And we're going to demo it at one of her tea dances.' He smiled. 'I did think it would be fun to do it at Blackpool Tower, given it's the most famous ballroom in the country, but we can't make the schedule or the budget work.'

'That's a shame,' she said. 'But a tea dance demo sounds fun. I was wondering where you planned to do the dances you've learned—I think you definitely need a proper audience, after all that hard work, not just a TV camera.'

'I'll see what my experts suggest,' he said. 'What are you planning for me?'

'I'm still thinking about it,' she said. 'Actually, I'm seeing Judith Parrish later today, to discuss music and choreography. She might have some ideas.'

He'd finished his third bacon roll and a bowl of yogurt and berries when he realised he needed to leave, or he'd be late for his interview.

'Sorry. I should've stopped talking and done the washing up earlier,' he said.

She brushed it aside. 'It's fine. It'll take me two minutes. *Go*.'

'I'll call you later,' he promised.

It was late by the time Rory finished, that evening, and called Pippa. 'Sorry. I know you're back at work tomorrow, so I won't suggest going out for a drink,' he said.

'It's fine. How did you get on with your ballroom dance teacher?' she asked.

'The interview was great. And she's taught me the first few steps. Did you know it was originally called "the Quicktime Foxtrot and Charleston"?'

'What a mouthful!' She laughed. 'It'd take you nearly as long to say it as to dance it. Are you enjoying it?'

'It's fun,' he said. 'Though it really is quick. I'm not going to need cardio at the gym while I'm learning this.'

'Good,' she said.

'How did you get on with Judith?'

'We had a really good time. We've got some ideas for the new choreography. I don't really want to tell you anything about it, though, because I'd like it to be a surprise,' she said.

'I hate surprises,' he said.

She laughed. 'Tough. I'm still not telling you.'

* * *

Over the next couple of weeks, Pippa and Rory fell into a routine of snatching breakfast together in the café round the corner from the Fitzroy on the days she was working, and Rory went to three of Kenzo's classes a week. By tacit agreements, on Saturday nights, he cooked dinner and she stayed over at his; on Sundays, they did something together where wasps were unlikely to bother them; and on Sunday nights he stayed at hers.

Even though Rory kept telling himself this was a temporary fling, it was starting to feel like more than that. It felt like a real relationship. And it terrified him how easy and natural he found it to be with her—how quickly they'd adjusted to each other's quirks. How much he looked forward to seeing her. She was the highlight of his day.

Was it the same for her, too?

And did she, too, wonder how hard it would be to lose this from their lives when his documentary had finished, she'd got her promotion, and they'd gone their separate ways?

He wasn't going to ask her, because the answer was almost as scary as the question. So he kept their conversation light, that evening, when she asked him how the documentary was going.

'I'm doing the quickstep as a demo at a tea

dance; a tango, as part of a show; and the disco routine in a competition.'

'That all sounds great.' She smiled. 'I hope I get to see the dancing live, and not just the filmed versions.'

'I'll see what I can do. Obviously it depends on whether it fits in with your performances,' he said. 'Have you decided what you want me to do with the ballet routine?'

'I think you need to do a show for ballet, too. And we'll up the stakes so it's a challenge for both of us.' She looked at him. 'Dance for the audience at the Fitzroy.'

He shook his head. 'Even if you put me in a really minor part, I'm not going to be up to the standard to join your company in *Swan Lake*.'

'You're not going to be dancing in *Swan Lake*,' she said with a smile. 'We've got a month before the gala show. I know it means you'll be learning other routines with other dances at the same time, but I think you're capable of doing it without confusing your steps. And if we do thirty minutes every day you'll learn the routine better than if we concentrate your training over a whole day every week.'

'But Nathalie's already sorted out what's in the gala, hasn't she?' he asked.

'That's the thing about galas. We're performing favourite pieces from lots of ballets rather than staging one single ballet, so we can be flexible with what we're including and the running order.' She looked at him. 'If Judith's willing to come and play, that'd be another famous name as a draw for both the gala and your show. We'd be able to offer the world premiere of a new piece, and a famous TV presenter as a guest dancer; and if Kenise films it your show can use that as well as your performance.'

'I'm not *that* famous,' he said. 'And I'm not a dancer.'

'Not a dancer *yet*,' she corrected. 'We're working on that. And you are famous,' she reminded him. 'You have a prime-time Friday night slot. OK, so it's on one of the smaller channels, but it's still prime time. People know who you are. Dancing at the Fitzroy is going to get publicity for your documentary, and people are going to tune in to find out what it's all about.'

'Supposing Nathalie says yes. What do I dance?' he asked.

'One of the big solos—maybe the Sugar Plum Prince variation,' she said, and found a video of it for him on her phone.

He watched it in horror. 'No way am I ever going to be able to do all those leaps and pirouettes, even if I did it on a trampoline.'

'I was going to simplify it for you,' she said.

'You can still get the feel of the piece and tell the story, at your own level. How about a male version of the "Dying Swan"?'

She found him another clip. And that one was even scarier.

'That's very…gymnastic,' he said, trying to be diplomatic. 'I'm nearly thirty—not as flexible as I was when I was a teenager. Besides, in all the other episodes, I'm dancing with the person who taught me, not doing a solo.'

She coughed. 'Well, it'd be a bit difficult to do a quickstep routine or a tango on your own.'

'I think I should dance with my ballet teacher,' he said.

Which sounded a bit better than *I want to dance with you*, which was what he really wanted to say.

'Let me think about a routine,' she said. 'We need something where you're not going to lift me. Which isn't me being fussy or saying you're a weakling—it's…' She drummed her fingers on the table, clearly trying to think of how to phrase it. 'If you put your partner down wrong, there's the risk of a potential fracture. I don't want to put that kind of pressure on either of us.'

'Then why do they allow the celebs to do lifts in shows like *Strictly*?' he asked.

'Lifts are only allowed in some dances,' she

pointed out. 'And ballroom dance lifts aren't quite as high as the ones in ballet.'

'So no lifts.' And it was weird how disappointing that felt, to know that he couldn't dance ballet *properly* with her.

Maybe his disappointment showed in his voice, because she said, 'You can still dance something fabulous. I'll tweak things so it's lower risk for both of us, and it'll still be a challenge for you.'

They were curled up together on his sofa, the following Sunday afternoon, when the idea came to Pippa. *'Carmen.'*

'Carmen? I thought that was an opera?' Rory said, looking confused.

'It's a ballet as well. "Habanera" would be great. You'll know the music.' She hummed the tune and was pleased to see the recognition on his face.

'So what's the ballet about?' he asked.

'The same as the opera. Carmen's a free spirit; Don José, one of the soldiers, falls in love with her, but she falls in love with the bullfighter Escamillo. They end up in a love triangle; there are a few fights; and, at the end...' She wrinkled her nose. 'Don José kills Carmen.'

'So it's your typical ballet-cum-opera tragedy,' he said.

'Pretty much,' she said. 'But the "Habanera" bit isn't tragic. It's where you see Carmen all bright and sparkly. I like the version where she's in jail and Don José's trying to resist her but falls for her. The two dancers share the spotlight and there are no lifts, but you'll do some flashy-looking turns.' She grinned. 'And you'll get to look *very* sexy in a soldier's outfit.'

'What about you? What does Carmen wear?' he asked.

'A little black dress. Let me show you the clip,' she said. 'Though you need to see this on a big screen. I want you to really see what's happening and feel all the feels, as it were.'

'We can connect the phone to the TV,' he said. Between them, they sorted it out and he came to sit beside her on the sofa.

She pressed 'play', and the music spilled into the air. Carmen, in handcuffs, danced lightly in and out of the bars, while Don José tried to ignore her and do his duty as a brave soldier—but gradually he began to follow her lead, and finally she walked free while Don José remained behind bars, wearing her handcuffs and looking as if he didn't understand what had just happened.

'Oh, my God,' Rory said, his voice husky. 'That has to be one of the sexiest…'

'Want to dance it with me?' she asked.

'Definitely,' he said. 'But is it too…well, *hot*, for a gala show? I don't want to embarrass either of us.'

The way he kissed her then left her in no doubt of his feelings.

'You have a point,' she said. 'The other piece I was considering—well, it makes me a bit twitchy even suggesting it.'

His blue eyes glinted. 'Tell me anyway. I won't take offence.'

'There's a gorgeous version of the "Rose Adagio" in *Sleeping Beauty*,' Pippa said. 'Instead of the Princess dancing with the four different suitors—which is the traditional one—she finds someone she's really attracted to, and dances with him in the garden. He's pretty much forbidden to her, and they both know it, but they can't help their feelings. It's glorious. I know it's a bit longer than you originally wanted, but I think it's worth it. Let me show you the first half.' She found the clip, and they watched it together.

'I get exactly what you mean. The Princess falls in love with the gardener,' he said. 'I love how they're teasing each other with the roses. It's like the first time you fall in love with someone, all the fizziness and dizziness.'

Which was the way she was starting to think about Rory—and that was seriously scary.

'But it has all those lifts,' he said.

'We'll replace them with turns,' she reassured him.

'I don't get why you were twitchy about suggesting it,' he said.

'It's the second half.' She pressed 'play' again.

'Instead of pricking her finger on a spindle, she pricks her finger on a rose…and dies,' he realised at the end. 'Back at the time this was set, there were no antibiotics. You could die from pricking your finger on a rose.'

'That's what made me twitchy,' she said. 'You were stung by a wasp, and you almost…' She felt tears pricking her eyes at the idea of a world without Rory in it. 'It's a bit too close to the bone.'

'But there's a happy ending. Everyone knows that, in the end, Sleeping Beauty's woken by true love's kiss,' he said. 'And I woke up, too, thanks to you—because you gave me the kiss of life.'

'Mmm,' she said, not quite trusting herself to speak.

'You know what? That'd be a lovely story in my series as well as for the gala,' he said. 'And afterwards, after you "die" on stage, I can tell the story of how you saved my life. The audience will love it.'

'So we're going for the "Rose Adagio"?' she asked.

'The "Rose Adagio",' he confirmed. And then he gave her the wickedest grin she'd ever seen. 'As long as you do the "Habanera" with me privately.'

'I will.' She returned the grin. 'And that's a promise.'

CHAPTER TEN

PIPPA COULDN'T REMEMBER being this happy. She loved her job, she loved her life, and she loved seeing the way Rory was falling in love with all forms of dance. He was teaching her a different way of looking at things, too—something which she hoped was filtering through to the way she did her job, enriching it.

What she hadn't expected was to adore the challenge of adapting choreography for a beginner and teaching Rory to dance. Nathalie had agreed to let Pippa perform the premiere of her *Four Seasons* piece with Judith at the gala performance, as well as dancing the rechoreographed version of the 'Rose Adagio'—and, even better, she'd agreed to let Rory film both pieces for his documentary.

He'd said to Pippa that they were on the same side. More than that, she thought; they'd become a team. Trusting each other. Letting each other in, admitting their fears. Seeing each other for who they were, flaws and all. His job and his position as the son of an earl weren't important to her at all; it was the man himself she liked. The man who made her laugh with terrible jokes. She liked him. *Really* liked him. To the point where she was beginning to hope that their fling wasn't just going to fizzle out— that they could build on it and make it work.

She'd always thought that love wouldn't happen for her. That there wasn't space in her life, because she couldn't risk letting someone distract her from getting to the top in her career. But Rory made her wonder if things could be different. There was no pressure. He didn't make her feel as if she was letting him down. And he wasn't distracting her—if anything, she was dancing better than she'd ever danced before.

Could they make something more from their fling?

With the right person, could she make space in her life and have ballet *and* a partner?

Could Rory be her Mr Right?

Before they started training, Pippa took Rory to her usual dance supplier and found him some black canvas ballet shoes, as well as a dance belt. He looked horrified when the assistant brought it out. 'It's like a G-string!'

'Which means it won't show through your

dance tights,' she said. 'And yes, you do need to wear one—firstly to support your anatomy, and secondly to protect you from injury. You wouldn't play cricket without a box, would you?'

He rolled his eyes, but agreed and tried them on until he had the right fit.

She enjoyed teaching him the foot and arm positions followed by the basic steps, especially when his confidence grew enough that she could name a step and he could do it without needing her to remind him with a prompt. She was pleased to note that he was quick at picking up the combinations.

It probably helped that they practised every day; on days when Pippa wasn't dancing Odile/ Odette, they used one of the practice rooms at the Fitzroy to run through their tweaked version of the Rose Adagio, polishing each section before moving to the next and then recapping everything they'd done so far. And at weekends they pushed the furniture back in his living room, rolled up the rug and danced there.

She hadn't seen as much as she would've liked to of Rory's dance diaries, but luckily the afternoon of the tea dance had been on a day when she hadn't been needed for rehearsals and actually had some free time, so she'd seen his quickstep routine performed live. Plus she'd been able to attend the dress rehearsal of his tango—a gorgeous, sensual dance that he'd then re-enacted with her in his flat on the Saturday night. The disco competition hadn't worked out with her schedules, but he'd promised to let her see what they'd filmed. And they'd come second, which had thrilled him.

Teaching Rory had made Pippa more aware of the way she danced, and in the middle of their third week Nathalie took her to one side. 'Whatever you're doing,' she said, 'I approve. Because you're taking dance to the next level. Your Odile was always technically flawless, but now you're putting more of your heart into the performance.'

Because of Rory. Not that she could say that.

'I think it's teaching, and maybe the choreography, because it's given me a different view of how routines work,' Pippa said. 'There are a couple of bits I haven't quite sorted out yet, but I've switched most of the lifts to a turn.'

'Show me what you've got so far, and I'll see if I can help,' Nathalie said.

Rory was less keen when he arrived for practice and Pippa told him Nathalie was going to watch them. 'I'm not ready for an audience yet. What if I mess it up?'

'You smile and keep going,' Nathalie said. 'I'm sure there are times in front of a camera where you say "um" or the wrong word. You don't stop then, do you?'

'Actually, we do. We stop and redo a few sentences, and then I splice the right bits together afterwards,' Rory said.

'What about when you do live interviews?' Nathalie asked.

'You don't have a choice, then. You have to smile and keep going,' he admitted.

'*Exactement*. This is the same. Don't worry if you get a few steps wrong. It won't matter. I need to see the soul of the piece.' She flapped a dismissive hand. 'Now show me.'

'Breathe. *Smile*. You've got this,' Pippa said. 'You're the gardener, you've fallen in love with the Princess, and she dazzles you. The only thing you can see is her—just as you dazzle her and the only thing she can see is you.'

'Got it,' he said. 'We dazzle each other.' Then he grinned. 'I've been thinking about my ballet stage name. That could be it—Dazzle.'

'No,' she said.

'Or maybe that should be my disco name,' he mused, 'and I could be Rory Fan-Nureyev.'

She groaned. 'That's worse.'

'Wait until you hear the rest. Rory Fanstaire dances ballroom.' His grin broadened. 'And Rory Fandango dances the tango.'

She could see he was cracking terrible jokes

to cover his nerves, and she really wanted to kiss him better—but at the same time they'd agreed to keep their fling just to themselves. Kissing him in front of Nathalie would be a really bad idea. She didn't want her boss realising that things were changing between her and Rory, and assuming that Pippa's commitment to her work would start to slip.

'You're not Rory any more. You're the gardener,' she reminded him. And she was the Princess, falling in love with the gardener—except she was still Pippa. And, even though she was still keeping it to herself, she knew she was falling in love with Rory. 'Go sit on the bench.' She connected her phone up to the room's sound system, then went to sit on the bench with him. As the music started, she rested her head against his shoulder, and then they began the dance.

They ran through the routine with only a couple of stumbles.

'And here's my sticking point,' Pippa said. 'We're about three minutes in. This is where we're taking shelter in the greenhouse and the rain stops, and everyone comes back into the garden.' She frowned. 'It'd be too complicated to make it an ensemble piece.'

'There's a natural break in the music, so you could stop there,' Nathalie said.

'But then we've only told part of the story,'

Rory said. 'We've got that extra minute and a half, where they're still happy and madly in love—but then she pricks her finger on the rose and it all goes horribly wrong.'

'And the problem's that tiny bit in the middle,' Nathalie said. 'You're right—we can't bring in half a dozen dancers just for a few seconds. But maybe,' she added thoughtfully, 'you could use a projector to show people coming into the garden while the Princess and the gardener are in the greenhouse. Then the projection fades out again, and you dance the second part.'

'I guess it depends on the mood we want to create,' Pippa said. 'Do we stop with them both having just fallen in love, or do we go on to the moment tragedy seems to strike?'

'Everyone knows *Sleeping Beauty* has a happy ending—she doesn't die, and he wakes her,' Nathalie said. 'If you leave it in the middle, you're ending on an anticlimax. It's pretty, but nothing happens to make you want to know what comes next. I think you should go for the drama.'

'What do you think, Rory?' Pippa asked, wanting him to be part of the decision. 'It means a fair bit of work, learning another two minutes.'

'Let's do it,' he said.

'Good choice,' Nathalie said, smiling. 'I like what I've seen. I'm not going to comment on the bits that need polishing, because you know that for yourselves. You're doing all right, Rory.'

From the plain-speaking chief executive, that was a high compliment.

'I'll talk to Marcos in Lighting about a projector,' Nathalie continued. 'Decide what you want the crowd to do, Pippa, block it through, and we'll film it.'

'Thank you,' Pippa and Rory said at the same time.

'I think you've simplified it well, Pippa—even without the lifts you've got that sense of falling in love,' Nathalie said. 'Though I noticed that one lift you left in.'

The straddle over the back. Pippa knew her boss's feelings about taking risks, because Nathalie always hammered it home to the team. 'It's a tiny, tiny, *tiny* lift. And it's an easy one,' Pippa said. 'I'm confident about it because I've seen the lift Rory does in his tango.'

'All right, then. Though you're sensible to leave it at one,' Nathalie said.

'I'm not taking risks with either of us,' Pippa reassured her. 'That's why we're doing turns rather than lifts.'

Nathalie nodded. 'When do I get to see the piece you're doing with Judith Parrish?'

'End of the week. Rory's banned,' Pippa added. 'Judith and I have been doing a video diary with a bit of help from Kenise. But he doesn't get to see the files until after the gala.'

'Considering it's *my* documentary,' Rory said, 'I'm not very happy about that.'

'If you analyse it all the way through development, then the final piece won't have as much impact on you,' Pippa argued. 'My way, you already know the concept, but you see the final as a brand-new audience would, and *then* you can take it to pieces and look at the development.'

'That's a good approach,' Nathalie said.

'You're biased because you're her boss,' Rory grumbled.

'I'm her boss because I saw her potential and I hired her,' Nathalie retorted. 'Get on with your practising. I need this room in fifteen minutes.'

'Oui, madame,' Pippa said with a smile.

Rory had never been this happy. His whole life seemed to have changed since Pippa had saved it. Her working hours were as unsocial as you could get, but they'd managed to work their dates around it—meeting for breakfast instead of dinner, doing Kenzo's classes together, spending weekends catching up with his family and friends on Saturday, and doing normal 'couply' things with Pippa on Sundays. She liked art galleries and museums as much as he did; and he quickly found that he could talk to her about anything.

Because they'd agreed up front this was just a fling, with no expectations, he found himself relaxing instead of wondering when it was all going to go wrong, the way his relationships had in the past. And she seemed to be relaxed in his company, too.

The dizzy, fizzy feel to the *Sleeping Beauty* piece was how he was feeling about Pippa, too, but he wasn't going to say anything yet. He was starting to hope that maybe the bond they were building was one that could actually last; but what if he'd still got it wrong? What if she didn't feel the same? Would she walk away? He didn't want to risk jinxing it by admitting how he felt.

The following Sunday, they were having a lazy morning at his place when his doorbell rang.

Odd. He wasn't expecting visitors or a courier.

He opened the door to see Jamie, Lottie, their partners and all four children.

Oh, no.

Much as he loved his family, if he invited them in, he'd have to introduce them to Pippa.

But if he didn't invite them in, they'd assume something was wrong.

Why were they all here, anyway? Hadn't he reassured them enough that he was perfectly fine and wasn't going to take any risks?

'We just called round to see if you'd like to come out to lunch with us. A new café just opened and apparently they do the most amazing pancakes,' Jamie said.

'I...um...' *Come on, think.* But the words were stuck in his head.

'Too many cocktails last night?' Lottie teased.

'No, I...' He rubbed a hand across his eyes. There wasn't a choice. They'd have to meet her. 'Come in.'

'Sorry. I didn't realise you already had company,' Lottie said when she saw Pippa sitting on the sofa.

'We were just...uh—' Then he saw the cafetiere on the coffee table and the panic in his head eased. 'Catching up over coffee. Pippa, this is my brother Jamie and my sister-in-law Miranda, my sister Lottie and my brother-in-law Martyn, and my nieces and nephews—Phin's ten, Albert's seven, Sarah's five and Lydia's three.'

'Lydia—you're the baker with fabulous glitter, right?' Pippa asked, and the little girl nodded shyly.

'Everyone, this is Pippa Barnes. My friend,' he said.

'Don't be shy, Rory,' Pippa said, and for one brief, hope-filled moment he thought she was actually going to tell them they were dating.

'I'm becoming Rory's friend,' she said, 'but I'm teaching him a ballet routine for his TV series. See, I've got my pointe shoes with me.' She nodded to the shoes on top of their box, and Rory was really glad they'd done some practising earlier. 'We're practising here because Rory's house has enough room if we move the furniture.'

Of course she wasn't going to out them. She was telling the truth—just not the whole truth. Although he wasn't a fan of untruths, he knew this white lie would stop anyone getting hurt; it meant there was a good chance they'd get away with this and wouldn't be grilled over their relationship until they were ready to share. Most of him was relieved, but an irrational bit of him was disappointed that she'd dismissed their deeper connection so easily. That didn't bode well for the future.

Lottie frowned. 'Don't you have a studio where you teach him?'

'It's at the theatre, which isn't open on Sundays,' Pippa said. Rory knew this wasn't strictly true because she had a key and there was a rota where the dancers could book the studio rooms for practice.

'Hang on. Aren't you the one who saved Rory's life?' Jamie asked.

Pippa flapped a hand. 'That's all done and dusted. I'm busy teaching him how to be a ballet dancer, which is a lot harder.'

Neither Jamie nor Lottie looked convinced.

'Thank you for saving him,' Jamie said. 'I can't tell you how grateful we all are.'

'You don't need to,' Pippa said. 'And I wasn't the only one. There was Carolyn, who did the CPR with me, and the paramedics. It's honestly not a big deal.'

'It is to us,' Lottie said quietly.

'He's fine,' Pippa said. 'And when he's not, he can practise ballet—which is the best thing I know to help you chill out.' She smiled at Lydia. 'Now, young lady. Your uncle gave me one of your cupcakes—because it's always nice to give your teacher a little present—and it was awesome. I've danced in a tutu that colour and it had tiny silver star sequins, just like your sprinkles.'

'You were a fairy ballerina?' Lydia asked.

'The Sugar Plum fairy,' Pippa said with a smile.

'I want to dance like the Sugar Plum fairy,' Sarah said.

'Do you have lessons?' Pippa asked.

'No.' Sarah looked disappointed.

'I can teach you all a bit now,' Pippa offered, 'if you like and if your mums say it's OK.'

'It's fine,' Lottie said, 'as long as it's no trouble to you.'

'Fine by me, too,' Miranda said.

'But boys don't dance ballet,' Phin said, narrowing his eyes.

'Oh, yes, they do,' Pippa said. 'There are some productions of Swan Lake where all the swans are boys. They wear feathery trousers and they hiss, so they're scary. Dance isn't all about tutus and fairy wands—it's about telling a story. Sometimes it's a happy one and sometimes it's a sad one.'

'Do they really hiss?' Albert asked.

'Just like real swans do,' Pippa said. 'Do you want to try?'

Lydia, Sarah and Albert all started hissing.

'That's brilliant,' she said, smiling. 'Now, have a think about how little swans move. What do you think they do? Do they glide, like their mum and dad—' she demonstrated '—or are they still a bit wobbly because they're babies?'

'Wobbly!' Lydia cried, and did her best to waddle. Her sister and Albert followed suit.

'That's perfect,' Pippa said. 'Phin, you're older.

How would a swan who's nearly old enough for the swan equivalent of big school move?'

Phin shrugged.

'I think,' she said, 'he tries to be all sensible and quiet because he thinks he's supposed to be like the grown-ups—but then he sees what fun his brother and cousins are having, hopping about. Do you think he'd just sit and watch with the adults, or do you think he'd join in with the little ones?'

Phin looked at her, saying nothing.

All the other adults were silent, wondering where this was going and if Phin was about to throw a pre-teenage hissy fit.

Pippa did a quick move Rory recognised as a pas de chat, then winked broadly. 'It's a lot more fun doing ballet than watching. Me, I'd rather be here being a wobbly cygnet—' she demonstrated '—than sitting still and sipping a cup of tea.' She mimed drinking from a porcelain cup with her little finger extended.

Phin was clearly thinking about it; finally, he nodded and went to join the others.

Rory almost sagged in relief. Pippa had managed to connect with his nephew. Then again, why had he doubted her? 'I'll make some coffee.'

'I'll help,' Martyn said.

'Right, gang. We're swans,' Pippa said. 'How do our heads move?'

They bobbed their heads, and even Phin joined in.

'Now, arms—they're wings. We can do big moves when we're flying through the sky—' she demonstrated dramatic arm movements '—or we can do little moves when we're gliding along the water.' She showed them little rippling movements with her arms.

Rory glanced at his siblings and their partners and saw they were all spellbound by Pippa. He knew this was going to be reported back to his mum and she'd start asking difficult questions, but right at that moment he didn't care; he just wanted them all to see Pippa the same way he did.

The children copied the swan arms, following Pippa's direction.

'There's a really famous dance about little swans. Can I teach you?' Pippa asked.

They all nodded enthusiastically, this time including Phin.

'Rory, can we have the carpet rolled back?' Pippa asked.

'Sure. We were going to do that anyway. And we'll move the tables,' he said, roping Jamie and his brother-in-law Martyn into helping him.

'Roll your socks down to the middle of your

foot, she said to the children. I want you to be able to glide, in some places, but I don't want you to slip, so you need to keep your heels bare to give you some grip on the floor.'

Rory loved how clear she was with her instructions, and the children were paying very close attention.

'We'll do the legs first, and when we've got that right we'll do the arms,' she said. 'Listen to the music and tap the beat with me with your right foot. One and two and three four five, and…' she counted.

'Semiquavers and rests,' Phin said laconically.

'Great—you're a musician!' Pippa said. 'What do you play?'

'Piano.'

'I love piano music,' Pippa said. 'Maybe you can play for me sometime.'

He blushed and nodded.

'What's your favourite piece?'

'I just did Grade Two,' he said. 'My teacher let me choose my favourite piece from each list. I did "Haggis Hunt", and "Hedwig's Theme".'

'I don't know "Haggis Hunt",' she said, 'but we sometimes use "Hedwig's Theme" as part of our warm-ups, and that's lovely.'

'I liked them a lot,' Phin said, 'but my favourite was Einaudi's "Snow Prelude"—it's like you're standing outside, looking up at the sky and seeing all the snowflakes swirl down around you.'

'It sounds like music for you is like dance is for me,' Pippa said. 'We're going to have some real fun now.'

She got the children to warm up their feet, then looked at Lottie and Miranda. 'You can come and join us, if you like.'

'No, no—we'll watch,' Miranda said, but she sounded wistful.

'If you want to stay in the audience, go and sit down. But any of you can hop up and join in at any time, and that's fine,' Pippa said. 'Just warm your feet up, first—like we're going to do.'

She took the children through some warm-up exercises, then taught them the basic footwork.

'Bravo,' she said, clapping. 'And now we add the arms. You're going to cross arms to do this, just like the little swans do on stage when we dance *Swan Lake*.'

The children immediately crossed their arms in the style of 'Auld Lang Syne'.

'That's good,' Pippa said, 'but ballet gives you a bit more movement, so you need a little bit more of a gap between you all. There's a trick to that—instead of holding the hand of the person next to you, you hold the hand of the person next to them. And then we tuck in nicely at each end.'

Within ten minutes, she had the children dancing up and down Rory's living room, then rising onto tiptoe and lowering back to flat feet, all in perfect time with the music.

'And that's it!' she said when the music ended. 'Take a bow—or a curtsey, and remember to smile at the audience,' she said to the children, clapping.

The adults all dutifully clapped.

'Well done, my little swans. You were excellent,' Pippa said. 'I'd better go now and let you have time with your family, Rory. We'll catch up with ballet practice tomorrow.'

'Don't go, Pippa,' Lottie said. 'Come for lunch with us.'

'I…' Pippa looked awkward.

Rory was about to step in with an excuse when Lottie asked, 'Unless you're busy?'

'Nothing that can't wait until tomorrow,' Pippa said. 'If you're sure—if you're not just being polite.'

'Very sure.'

When they went out to the café Jamie had mentioned, Rory noticed that Pippa ended up being sandwiched between Lottie and Miranda. And they were chatting as if they'd known each other for years.

'Stop worrying. Lottie's not going to grill her,' Jamie said, nudging Rory in the ribs.

'No need. Miranda will do that,' Martyn added, chuckling.

'Not funny,' Rory said. 'Pippa's my new colleague. Sort of. She really *is* teaching me to dance for the show.'

'The way you look at each other,' Jamie said softly, 'I think she's a lot more than that.'

Rory sighed. He should've known he couldn't quite get away with this. 'It's really early days. I don't want Mum putting any pressure on. As soon as you or Lottie tell her, she'll be planning a wedding.'

'We'll tell her,' Jamie said, 'but we'll also tell her to back off.'

Rory scoffed. 'As if that's going to work.'

'Oh, it will,' Martyn said. 'Lottie has other news to distract her.'

Rory felt his eyes widen as he guessed what Martyn meant. 'Seriously?'

'Shh,' Martyn said. 'Don't tell Lottie I told you. We're not supposed to be telling anyone until twelve weeks.'

'Congratulations,' Rory said.

And how weird was it that he felt wistful about his sister having another baby? He didn't do wistful. He enjoyed his nieces and nephews hugely, but he'd never thought about having children of his own. Probably because he'd never dated anyone he wanted to start a family with. And it worried him that Pippa was different—that, since being with her, he was starting to want different things from life.

'She's lovely,' Jamie said. 'She's not like the usual women you date. And she's brilliant with the kids. Phin's heading towards being a teenager, and I thought he was going to be in a sulk—but she made him feel part of everything. She really got him.'

'Yeah. She's special,' Rory said.

Jamie raised his eyebrows. 'That's what I said about Miranda,' he said gently. 'She wasn't like the women who looked at me and immediately saw themselves as the future Countess of Riverford. I take it Pippa knows who Mum and Dad are?'

'She does,' Rory said. 'And obviously she knows about my job.'

'We'll make sure Mum backs off,' Jamie said. 'Because, when you're ready to give us a sister-in-law, I think Pippa might be the one.'

CHAPTER ELEVEN

BROODY.

Rory had never, ever expected to feel broody.

The way he'd planned things, he was going to take a break from dating and concentrate on moving his career to the next level. Once he'd done that, he'd think about what he wanted in a partner and try to find someone who saw him for himself, not for his job or his background. All neat and tidy and sensible.

But then the wasp had happened, and his close brush with dying had made him question his choices. It had made him question *everything*.

He'd gone back to Plan A, but that surge of attraction towards Pippa had seriously got in the way. Their fling was supposed to be all about getting it out of their systems so they could be sensible again—but somehow it had turned into something else. Falling in love with her particular art form had gradually changed to falling in love with *her*.

Seeing Pippa with his nieces and nephews at the weekend and that unexpected conversation with his brother had crystallised something in his head. Now, he knew exactly what he wanted. Not just his career, but a family of his own. Children. And he wanted more than a short, intense fling with Pippa. He wanted her *permanently*. He wanted to plight his troth to her in front of all their family and friends. To love, honour and cherish her for the rest of their days. To watch her walk gracefully down the aisle to him, smiling behind her veil. To make a family with her. Cuddle their babies— and he'd do his fair share of changing nappies. Read their toddlers stories together, doing all the voices between them.

The problem was, how did that fit in with what *she* wanted from life?

He knew how much Pippa wanted this promotion. Even though he thought she'd made the right career choice, she still doubted herself and thought she'd let her family down. Reaching the peak of a dance career would prove to them, and her, that she'd been right not to become a doctor.

But promotion to principal dancer meant she might need to travel a lot more, touring and guest-starring with other ballet companies. None of that fitted with marriage and babies.

Did she even want children in the future? Then again, the way she'd been with his nieces and nephews, warm and inclusive…it made him hope that she did. Though they'd need to talk about it, and he definitely didn't want her to feel that she had to choose between her career and him. Ballet was a huge part of her life, and he wanted her to be happy.

So how could he convince her that they could find a compromise? That she could still do the job she loved, while having the family he wanted?

Rory tried to tamp down the feelings, not wanting to have the conversation before the gala and mess everything up, but the more he tried to suppress his feelings the more the longing seeped through.

Either he was doing a good job of hiding what was in his head, or she was so focused on the gala that she hadn't noticed how antsy he was. And then a really horrible thought struck him: maybe she *had* noticed. Maybe she'd worked it out. Maybe she didn't feel the same way he did, and was trying to work out how to let him down gently…

At last, it was Saturday night and the Fitzroy's Gala Show.

Rory and Pippa were dancing third.

The first piece was Yuki dancing the Sugar Plum Fairy; she was exquisite, and the audience clearly loved it.

The second piece was the 'Dance of the Little Swans'—another popular choice, but Rory found himself unable to focus. He was too aware of what was coming next.

Nathalie walked onto the stage with the microphone. 'I'm sure many of you know Pippa Barnes from her performances here. Tonight she'll be dancing with a television star I'm sure many of you know well too: Rory Fanshawe. Since she saved his life when a wasp sting nearly killed him, she's been teaching him to dance for a documentary he's working on. Tonight, they're going to perform a special version of the "Rose Adagio" from *Sleeping Beauty*.'

Rory was so full of nerves that he couldn't even stand still.

The worst thing was, he knew that both his family and Pippa's were in the audience. He hadn't introduced her to his parents yet, and she hadn't introduced him to hers—or to her sisters. What if he messed this up? What if he let her down? What if this was such a dreadful performance that it made Nathalie decide to give the promotion to Yuki rather than to Pippa?

He'd been so cavalier about this, so sure that his documentary would get her noticed and help with her promotion. How would he live with himself if the opposite happened? Because he wasn't a knight on a white charger, riding up to save the day and rescue the damsel. Pippa didn't need rescuing: she was doing perfectly fine on her own. He'd behaved like every other entitled, clueless male.

And she was so cool and calm and collected, it was unreal.

'Break a leg,' she said, and winked at him. 'You can do this, Rory Fan-Nureyev.'

Even the nickname—the one *he'd* made up to tease her—couldn't make him smile. Because now he had to go out on that stage and give the best performance of his life—a performance he wasn't entirely sure he could do.

'Ignore the audience. I'm the Princess. Dance with me. *Dazzle* me,' she whispered.

How did he do that? How? He'd forgotten every single step she'd taught him. Which leg was meant to go in front when he did the first turn? Where did the arms go? What if he tripped over his own feet—or, worse, tripped over hers and broke her ankle?

He was shaking as he walked across the stage. It was utterly ridiculous. He'd spent years in broadcasting and he was perfectly used to talking in front of an audience. He could've compered the show for Nathalie without the slightest hesitation, and he would've done it well, charming the audience and showcasing the dancers.

But it was one thing knowing that more than a million viewers would be tuning in to watch his Friday night programme, and quite another knowing that two thousand ballet fans were going to watch him dance right here and now *on this stage*.

With his show, he knew what he was doing. He knew he was good enough. With this, the stakes were higher—it was Pippa, not him, who'd lose out if he made a mistake.

The seconds dragged on and on as they walked to the bench. Every step felt like lead. Why had he talked her into dancing with him? Why hadn't he just done the really simple version of the 'Dying Swan'? Why had he had to show off?

Why was he the one facing the audience, when she was the professional dancer?

But then the harp signalling the beginning of the adagio rang out into the auditorium. The stage lights went up. She leaned across and rested her head on his shoulder. He tipped his to one side and rested it against hers. Breathe, breathe, port de bras—then she was lying on the bench with her head in his lap, and suddenly he was the gardener and she was the Princess.

The audience faded away. The spotlight was simply the sun coming out in the garden after the rainstorm. And they danced, flirted, came together for a hug and for him to offer her a red rose he'd magicked from nowhere, dipped away again…

They'd practised little and often, because she said he'd remember it better that way. And he discovered that she was right. They'd done this so often that he didn't actually have to think about it. All he had to do was let his muscles remember what happened along with each note in the music, let the Princess dazzle the gardener, and dazzle the Princess in return.

Every note of the music was full of yearning and sweetness. Rory loved every second of being with her in that pretty dress, with its frothy petticoats that spun as they turned. He loved running with her to shelter in the 'greenhouse'. Nathalie's projection idea worked perfectly with people strolling in the garden—and Carabosse was there, too, holding a black rose and bringing the hint of danger to come.

The projection faded, and he and Pippa went back to the bench. Pippa 'found' Carabosse's black rose they'd hidden in the bench earlier, and for a moment Rory heard the audience gasp in horror as they realised its significance.

One last fleeting dance of joy, of knowing they loved each other and thinking it was all going to be perfect, and then the Princess picked up the rose again, pricked her finger, and 'died' in the horrified gardener's arms.

The stage lights went out—and then he heard the applause. Way, way more applause than he'd had from an audience before. People calling, 'Bravo!' People cheering. People whistling and stamping their feet.

And when the lights came up again and he and Pippa stood in the middle of the stage, holding hands, he blinked into the lights and he could see the audience giving him a standing ovation.

She did the most graceful curtsey, and the applause was deafening.

And then she stepped to the side. 'Bow,' she whispered, and gestured with her hands to showcase him.

He bowed, and somehow the applause got even louder. Which was utterly insane, because he wasn't the ballet star.

He tried to remember what they'd practised. *Smile, wave and walk off the stage.*

He was smiling so widely that his face almost hurt.

'Well done. You were brilliant,' she whispered when they got into the wings.

'It was all you,' he said. 'I was so scared I

was going to mess everything up for you…'
And then, because he really couldn't help himself, he kissed her. Not as if she was the Princess and he was the gardener, but because Pippa
Barnes dazzled him more than anyone he'd ever
met and he'd really fallen in love with her. He
kissed her as if his entire life depended on it.

The rest of the show passed in a blur after that;
Rory watched from the wings, but he couldn't
take any of it in, beautiful as the music and the
dancing were.

And then it was time for Pippa's world première. The piece he hadn't seen or heard. He
slipped out of the wings and went to stand in
the side aisle, just behind Kenise and her camera, out of the way of the audience.

The stage crew moved the piano onstage, and
Nathalie introduced Judith.

'Tonight I have the pleasure of giving you
the world première of Pippa Barnes' ballet
Four Seasons, with an original score by award-
winning composer Judith Parrish—who will be
performing the music for us herself, tonight.'
Clearly the audience knew exactly who Judith was, too, because there were whistles and
cheers and loud applause.

The lights dimmed as Nathalie walked off,
then brightened to show Pippa crouched in

the centre of the stage, wearing a pale green calf-length chiffon overdress on top of a skin-tone leotard. She was slowly unfurling, like a spring flower; the solo piano sounded like dappled sunlight on a forest floor, quiet at first and then becoming louder as the flower grew. The music was beautiful, reminiscent of Einaudi. Even though he knew the concept of the piece, she'd refused to let him see her dance it or even see the costume until tonight, wanting him to get the full impact.

And wow.

This was a bravura performance. She gave everything to the dance, and she was spellbinding, drawing pictures in his head. Spring flowers all fresh and new, like the beginning of a love affair; the drowsy sensuality of a rose in full bloom; leaves falling in an autumn storm, like an argument; and finally winter frost in the morning sun, showing him that even at the end it was bright and sparkling.

It clarified for him what she brought to his life. Warmth, brightness, beauty. Letting her slip through his fingers would be a huge mistake, bringing nothing but regret. So he needed to be as brave as she was on the stage: he needed to tell her how he really felt. Maybe not tonight—there was too much going on—but he'd make sure they found the time during the week. And he'd open his heart to her.

The piece ended with Judith crashing the piano like thunder and Pippa with her arms up like a bolt of lightning, spinning round in a triple pirouette before gracefully ending.

The stage went dark for a moment, and when the lights came back up the audience gave her a rapturous reception. Including Rory, who went to the edge of the stage and handed her the huge sheaf of roses he'd arranged for Kenise to bring. 'You were *amazing*,' he said.

The rest of the company and the guests all came back on stage, to a standing ovation. Rory lost count of how many curtain calls there were.

Finally, Nathalie walked onto the stage again with her microphone. 'I'd like to thank you all for coming tonight,' she said. 'To thank our guest stars, our dancers, our wardrobe and stage crew, the lighting and sound technicians—all of you came together and made this a night to remember. And, between the ticket sales, donations tonight and the fundraiser, I'm delighted to say that we've raised enough money to fix the roof.'

The cheers, Rory thought, were enough to *raise* the roof.

'We have one last week of performances, and then we'll be back in the autumn,' Nathalie said.

'I hope we can welcome as many of you as possible—hopefully here, but if we have to work on another stage I'll let you all know where we are. We're the Fitzroy Ballet Company, and we appreciate every one of you. I wish you goodnight and a safe journey home.'

The lights went up in the auditorium, and the safety curtain rolled down.

CHAPTER TWELVE

ON WEDNESDAY MORNING, Nathalie called Yuki and Pippa into her office between class and rehearsals. 'We've made a decision about the promotion to Principal Dancer,' she said. 'We've been talking about it, and we think you equally deserve the position.'

Pippa tensed. Nathalie wouldn't tell them both at the same time, would she? Surely she'd tell them separately? They both wanted the position, and it was going to be really hard for the one who didn't get it.

'We're promoting you both,' Nathalie said. 'Congratulations.'

It took a moment to sink in.

Yuki had got the promotion.

And so had she.

Yuki looked as stunned as she felt. For a moment, neither of them moved, as if moving would break the dream and wake them; then Pippa flung her arms round Yuki, and then they both hugged Nathalie.

'Thank you,' Pippa said. 'You have no idea how much this means.'

'Me, too,' Yuki said. 'I think this is the happiest day of my life.'

'We'll make the formal announcement on Saturday night, at the end of the show,' Nathalie said. 'I trust both of you can keep it secret until then?'

'Can I tell my mum?' Yuki asked. 'She'll keep it to herself. But she's supported me all the way through my career—I feel she's worked for this as much as I have.'

'Of course you can tell your closest family—both of you,' Nathalie said. 'But not a word to anyone else until Saturday night. And make sure they know they have to keep it quiet, too.'

'Of course,' Pippa said, and left Nathalie's office, looking as insouciant as she could.

She'd done it.

She'd made it to the top of the tree. Principal Dancer, at the age of twenty-five and with a non-conventional route into her career.

All the hours she'd put in—they'd been worth every single second.

And there was one person who'd really get how she felt, who'd feel the same delight that she did in her news. Especially because he'd admitted after the Gala Show how scared he'd been of failing and messing up her chances. He hadn't failed, and neither had she. She couldn't wait to share this with him.

Pippa grabbed her phone, opened the text app to bring up Rory's name—and then it hit her.

She couldn't tell him yet.

Enough people had witnessed their kiss in the wings at the Gala Show for everyone in the company to know now that they were an item; but she was pretty sure that Nathalie wouldn't class Rory as family. Plus he was a journalist. What if he accidentally let it slip to his editor, who insisted on him breaking the news on his show on Friday night—the day before Nathalie made the announcement? Even though Pippa trusted him, she knew Nathalie was right; the more people who knew, the more likely it was that the news would leak.

Instead, she texted her sisters and her mum.

TOP SECRET—will be announced Saturday after the show. Am not allowed to tell anyone except closest family. You're not allowed to tell anyone either. I GOT THE PROMOTION!!!!

It didn't feel quite the same. But they'd be pleased for her—wouldn't they?

Rory made the last adjustments to the ballet episode, then settled back to watch the whole thing again and double-check he was happy.

He was pretty sure he had the balance right. After the show, Kenise had given him the tapes she'd taken of Pippa and Judith's collaboration—which Pippa had insisted needed to be top secret—and he'd spliced the relevant bits in after the footage from the Gala Show. Because Pippa was right: it had much more impact if he saw the whole piece and then analysed it.

He paused after the Sleeping Beauty section, rewound, and watched it again.

They'd definitely caught the feeling of falling in love, the excitement and the way nothing else mattered except being together. Even without the lifts, her choreography had been clever enough to bring out all the emotion. And she was right—this dance wasn't just showcasing the Princess, it was both of them together.

This was something to be proud of. Something that one day, if they were lucky, they could show their children. Well, he didn't actually know if Pippa wanted children, and she'd been clear that her career was her priority for the next few years. He was getting ahead of himself. But at the same time he couldn't help wanting everything with her.

Acting was part of dance; but he didn't think that Pippa was simply telling the Princess's story, here. That dance had been about them, too. About the way they'd fallen in love. Although they hadn't discussed it, he was sure she felt the same way he did: that their fling had moved on, turned into something deeper and much more real. Something that could last.

Even though they hadn't scheduled meeting tonight, he couldn't wait until breakfast tomorrow. He needed to see her. Needed to tell her how he felt. Needed to ask her to take a chance on him.

He managed to get a last-minute ticket for *Swan Lake*; even though it was up in the gods and his view wasn't great, he didn't mind because it meant he got to see her dancing. Tonight she was dancing Odile/Odette, and he loved every second she was on stage.

At the end of the show, he made his way down to the stage door. From his time working with Pippa at the theatre, everyone at the Fitzroy knew him, and the security team just smiled and waved him in.

A few minutes later, Pippa came out of the dressing room with several of her colleagues, chatting and laughing. 'Rory! Hello. I wasn't expecting to see you tonight,' she said, smiling at him. 'We were just heading off for pizza. Guys—do you mind if Rory comes, too?'

'Of course not,' Livvy, one of the other dancers, said. 'He's practically one of us, now he's danced on our stage.'

'And you did so well on Saturday night. Give us a year, and we could get you doing lifts,' Teodoro, one of the other dancers, said.

'I wouldn't dare. I'd be terrified of dropping someone,' Rory said. 'Guys, can we catch up with you in a second? I just wanted a quick word with Pippa. About the filming,' he improvised.

'Sure. We'll go ahead and grab our table. Come when you're ready. Shall we order your usual for both of you, Pippa?' Livvy asked.

'Is *funghi di bosco* pizza OK with you?' Pippa checked.

'Sure,' he said.

Once the others had gone on, Pippa asked, 'Is there a problem with the film?'

Her expression added, *Something so terrible that you needed to tell me tonight instead of waiting until breakfast tomorrow morning?*

'No. I really enjoyed the video diary you did with Judith and Kenise,' he said. 'And you were absolutely right about making me wait to see the première first.'

'Then what did you want to talk about?' she asked.

'I've watched our performance from the Gala Show,' he said.

'Ye-es,' she said. 'You let me come into the studios to watch it with you on Monday.'

'I've watched it several times since then,' he said. 'And I think it works because it isn't just the gardener and the Princess falling in love.' This was the biggest risk he'd ever taken in his life. And he hadn't scripted it. He just hoped she'd know that the words were coming straight from his heart. 'It's me falling in love with you, for real.'

She stared at him, those storm-grey eyes huge.

'I know we said we were just going to have a fling and get it out of our systems, but that hasn't happened for me. I love you, Pippa. I never expected this to happen, but I really love you. The more I see you, the more I want to be with you. I'd kind of got lost in my head, after the wasp thing, questioning everything—but being with you changed that. I know what I want, especially after seeing the way you were with my nieces and nephews. I want *you*. And children, if we're lucky.' He dropped to one knee. 'I haven't bought a ring. Partly because I think we should choose it together, and partly because I just couldn't wait a second longer to ask you. That's why I came here tonight. Will you marry me, Pippa? Be my love, my wife, the heart of my family?'

Pippa stared at him in shock.

Marry him.

Have children.

But…she couldn't. Not now. She hadn't had the chance to tell him yet about her promotion—but now was completely the wrong time for her to get married, have a career break and have babies. The next five or ten years were the peak time for her career.

And even if she did manage to juggle babies and her career, what about Rory? His career was taking off, too. His documentary series would bring him to the attention of arts editors on other channels. He'd have opportunities he'd want to take. If they both focused on their careers, they'd be letting their children down. If she focused on her career, she'd be letting him down.

He wanted a family. He wanted children.

She'd seen how close he was with his nephews and nieces. He'd definitely be a hands-on father; but did he want children enough to be the parent who took the career break, the parent who worked from home and put their job second?

She'd spent years feeling that she'd let her parents down. Today, when Nathalie had called her into the office, was the first time she'd really felt validated—and even that was a bit wobbly, because her mum still hadn't replied to the text she'd sent about her promotion. Her sisters had both replied, messages full of emojis and exclamation marks, along with plans to celebrate at the weekend with champagne. But her parents clearly still felt she'd let them down, to the point where they were having to force themselves to congratulate her.

She didn't want to spend the rest of her life feeling she'd let Rory down, too—either making him wait years for the children he wanted, or making him put his career on hold so she could progress hers.

She had a choice to make: love, or her career.

Whichever one she chose, she'd lose the other.

If she told him her worries, he'd tell her they could work it out. But Rory was a wordsmith, and he was from a privileged background. He'd never really had to struggle for anything. He hadn't exactly been handed his career on a platter—he'd worked hard and he was good at his job—but with a career in media you needed a lucky break as well as talent. He'd had the contacts to give him that first break. He'd tell her that everything was fine...

But how could it be?

In ballet, if you took a break you'd be forgotten. She needed a good couple of years as Principal Dancer to make her name before she could take a break. She'd be doing guest spots with other companies, as well as dancing at the

Fitzroy—and that would mean long hours and lots of travelling. That didn't fit well with babies and young children—she'd hardly get to see them, or Rory. She'd be a failure both as a partner and as a parent.

On the other hand, if she gave up her career, would she start to regret all the might-have-beens? Would she even start to resent Rory and the children, blame them for the choice she'd made?

'Pippa?' He looked up anxiously at her. 'Will you marry me?'

Her throat dried.

Whatever she said would hurt him. Asking for time to think about it would only prolong the agony.

To be fair to both of them, there was only one answer she could give.

'I'm sorry,' she said. 'No.'

No.

She'd said no.

And it felt as if all the air had been sucked out of the room.

Rory stared at her. 'No?'

'No,' she said. 'I can't marry you.'

Couldn't, or *wouldn't*? Though that was splitting hairs. The end result was the same. She'd said no.

And it hurt.

It felt worse than that white-hot throbbing pain when the wasp had stung him, the wooziness and everything going black.

At least that had only been temporary. The sore spot on his neck and the burn mark on his chest from the defibrillator had become less painful, with regular application of aloe vera. They'd faded, leaving nothing more than a memory.

But there was a big difference between a physical pain and this, the feeling that something had just crushed his ribs and everything underneath them had turned into rubble. This was the kind of pain he didn't think would ever go away.

He'd made the most stupid mistake of his life: thinking that this time it would be different, because she saw him for who he was. But in the end it had been the same old, same old: he'd been the one who'd invested in the relationship, and his partner hadn't. Yet again he'd fallen for someone who didn't love him back. Someone who didn't want him. He'd opened his heart, bared his feelings—and she'd said no.

'I'm sorry,' she said again.

This wasn't how it was supposed to happen. In his head, she'd said yes, he'd picked her up and spun her round and made sure he set her back gently on her feet, and they'd kissed until they were dizzy, and it was all going to be the happiest ever after.

In real life, she'd said no, and he was down on one knee, feeling like the biggest fool in the world.

'I'm sorry, too,' he said quietly. He wasn't going to make even more of a fool of himself by asking why she'd turned him down. She'd made it very clear she didn't want him. What was the point in dragging it out? The simple facts were that he'd changed his mind about their fling, and she hadn't.

He got to his feet. 'I'll…um…'

No. He wouldn't see her around. *Have a nice life* sounded too bitter. All his skill with words seemed to have drained away, along with what was left of his heart.

In the end, he said lamely, 'Bye, then.'

'Rory,' she said as he turned to leave. 'Rory.'

But there was nothing she could say to make this better. He didn't want to hear it, so he didn't stop to listen. He put one foot in front of the other, mentally gritted his teeth, and walked away.

CHAPTER THIRTEEN

PIPPA WATCHED RORY LEAVE, feeling as if she'd been soaked in a downpour, wrung out, and left in a heap on the floor.

Though it was her choice.

She'd picked her career, not love. She'd been the one to turn him down, so she was just going to have to make the best of it.

But tonight she couldn't face being in anyone else's company.

She texted Livvy, the colleague who'd offered to order the pizzas for her and Rory.

Sorry to back out at last minute. Have awful headache. If too late to cancel our pizzas will settle up with you tomorrow, P xx

And then she slipped out of the stage door.

Today should've been the best day of her life—well, second-best day, because Saturday was the day that made her promotion official.

But she couldn't ever remember feeling this miserable and hopeless before.

But what other choice could she have made?

If she'd said yes—become Rory's wife, his equal partner, the mother of his children—she would've had to give up everything she'd worked for. And her sisters were right about her being a horrible workaholic; it was simply who she was. She couldn't change. She would've resented Rory for holding her back—or, if she'd made him wait for years before they started the family he wanted, she would've felt that she'd let him down. And she was so *tired* of feeling that she'd let people down.

She slept badly, claimed she'd been fighting off a headache when everyone expressed concern at how awful she looked, the next morning, gritted her teeth and just got on with her job.

But even when the card from her parents arrived—a beautiful line drawing of a ballerina on the front, and the words she'd longed to hear for so many years, written in her mother's tiny difficult-to-read doctor's handwriting, inside—it didn't lift her heart.

Congratulations on being promoted to Principal Dancer. What an achievement, and very much deserved. We're both so proud of you.

But I'm not proud of me, she thought. *I hurt Rory. He didn't deserve that.*

No matter which way she looked at it, she couldn't see another way. Whatever she'd done, he would've ended up hurt. Better to end it now than slowly and more soul-destroyingly. If that was even a word. Oh, for pity's sake, she couldn't even string a sentence together. He would've known what to say. Rory, who always finished her crosswords, who knew a poem or a Shakespeare quote for every eventuality under the sun, who could charm the moon with his words.

He'd charmed her.

The brightness he brought with him, the way he showed her to look at paintings in a different way, the way he'd become captivated by ballet. In their practice sessions, he'd worked and worked and worked until he got it right. He'd listened to her. He'd done everything she'd asked of him. He'd stepped out of his comfort zone for her. He'd walked out on that stage, and she'd seen how nervous he was, but he'd danced. For *her.*

She'd fallen in love with him, too.

And part of her had wanted so desperately to say yes to his proposal. To be with him. Her husband, her life, the heart of her family.

The way she'd been with his nieces and nephews, drawing out Phin's love of music and Lydia's love of putting sprinkles on cake, teaching all of them to dance like little swans: that morning had put a dream in her head, too. Of teaching her own children to dance, with Rory there, joining in or directing with his broadcast journalist hat on.

But she couldn't have it all. Nobody could. You had to make sacrifices along the way. She'd learn to cope with the collateral damage to her own heart; she just wished she hadn't damaged his.

The rest of the week was hideous. Even Saturday, when Pippa knew Nathalie was going to make the big announcement after the show, felt as flat and stale as champagne left out in a glass overnight.

And she couldn't stop thinking about Rory. Feeling guilty for hurting him, and missing him at the same time.

'The show must go on,' she reminded herself fiercely. One last performance as Odette/Odile, and then she'd have a break over the summer. Maybe she'd take her sisters up on their offer of going to France with them. Getting out of London, where there were way too many memories of Rory, might help.

At least she was dancing *Swan Lake*, not *Sleeping Beauty*.

Rory had been spot-on in that. It had worked so well precisely because it was real, not just acting. She'd gloried in dancing with the man she'd fallen in love with, knowing that he loved her too, even though neither of them had declared their feelings. If she ever had to dance that with anyone else, it would break her.

Though it distracted her to the point where in Act Three, at the very end of Odile's triumphant dance, she felt herself slip.

Felt the wrench on her ankle.

Heard the pop.

Knew she'd done something serious.

She stayed in pose, as required; then managed to walk off stage through the pain. But the second she was in the wings, out of sight off the audience, she stopped and unlaced her pointe shoe.

Her ankle was definitely swelling. And it really hurt to put weight on it.

'Are you all right? What happened?' Yuki asked, hurrying over to her.

'I don't know.' Pippa blinked back the tears. 'I'm not sure if it's a sprain.'

'Can you walk?' Yuki asked.

Pippa tried again, and was shocked by how much more painful it was this time to put weight on her ankle. 'I can walk, but I'm not sure I can dance,' she said bleakly.

'Pippa?' Nathalie bustled over. 'What happened?'

'I slipped. I…' She couldn't bail out of the last act. She had to do this for the good of the company. She took a deep breath. 'I'll be OK. I'll take ibuprofen and ice my ankle while I'm in the wings.'

Nathalie examined her ankle. 'I'm not a medic, but I don't think you've broken your ankle. Though I've seen enough ligament tears to recognise one—if you dance on this, you're risking permanent damage. And that's not happening in my company.' She snapped her fingers. 'Yuki, you're taking over now as Odette. Livvy, I need you to dance Yuki's part in the "Two Swans". Go and get changed!' She looked at Pippa. 'And *you* are going straight to the hospital.'

So she wouldn't even be here when her promotion was announced. *If* it was still announced. If Nathalie was right and she'd torn a ligament, it could be months and months before she was fit enough to dance again.

'I—' she began.

'No arguments,' Nathalie said firmly. 'Your health is important. Go, *petite*.'

'I'll go with you,' Aeris, one of the junior

dancers who was watching from the wings, offered.

It was a long, long wait. Aeris did her best to keep Pippa chatting and distracted as they waited for a doctor to see her, but all Pippa could think about was what damage the doctors would find and how long she'd be out of dance.

And the MRI scan gave the worst news.

'It's a grade three ligament tear,' the doctor said.

'Does that mean surgery?' Pippa asked.

'For people who aren't elite athletes or dancers, it's an injury that would heal without surgery,' the doctor said. 'But, given your job, you'll want to be back at peak fitness like yesterday. I think you'd be better off with surgery, a cast, and physio. But you'll need to be careful in rehab—don't try to be brave and work through the pain, because you'll do more damage and slow your recovery down.'

'How much time are we looking at until I can dance properly again?' Pippa asked, needing to know the worst.

'Six months.'

Six months?

It sounded like a lifetime.

There was no way she'd keep her promotion, now. Not only that, she'd lose ground, and this meant six months out of the most crucial years of her career. Everything she'd worked for was slipping away, and there wasn't a thing she could do about it.

'We'll immobilise your foot for now,' the doctor said, 'and we'll operate in the morning. Provided there aren't any complications, you can go home tomorrow afternoon.'

Even though it was late, the theatre director had said she wanted to know as soon as there was any news, so Pippa phoned her.

'That's not as bad as it sounds,' Nathalie said. 'We're having two months off for the summer, while the roof's being fixed. You're only missing four months.'

Only.

'And I'm sure Rory can distract you for those four months,' Nathalie added.

Ri-i-i-ight. Rory distracting her was why she was in this mess in the first place.

Pippa closed her eyes. No, that wasn't fair. It wasn't his fault. It was all on her. And it was her fault she'd let the Fitzroy down. 'He won't be distracting me,' she said. 'We won't be seeing each other again.'

'That,' Nathalie said, her voice carefully neutral, 'is a shame. I liked him.'

The lack of judgement, the kindness, was almost Pippa's undoing. 'I'll be back to work in six months,' she said. 'I assume you didn't announce my promotion. I mean, you can hardly promote someone who can't even do the job right now.'

'It's my company,' Nathalie reminded her, 'so I can do what I like. As a matter of fact, I announced Yuki's promotion *and* yours at the end of the show. And if it takes more than six months for you to be back to full fitness on my stage, then it takes more than six months.'

'You're not sacking me?' The words spilled out before Pippa could stop them.

'You can't sack someone for illness,' Nathalie said. 'Though, even if it was legally allowed, it would be totally amoral and I wouldn't do it.'

'What if I…?' Pippa forced herself to say the words, to face the issue. 'What if I never get back to full fitness?'

'Don't overthink it,' Nathalie said sternly. 'Focus on the positives. You'll have the surgery, we have an excellent physio who can help you with rehab exercises, and…' She paused. *'Qui vivra, verra.'*

But what if the damage was too much? Pippa wondered. What if she couldn't dance any more?

She'd chosen her career over Rory. If she lost her dancing, too, then she'd lost everything.

Unable to face any further conversations, she

told her sisters the news by text. Telling her parents was too much to handle; she'd do it after the operation, she decided. So she was truly shocked when, at seven o'clock the next morning, her mother walked onto the ward.

'Mum! I— What are you doing here?'

'Supporting you,' her mother said. 'I assume you're nil by mouth?'

Pippa nodded.

'Right. If you give your permission for your doctors to talk to me, I can make sure they're taking the best approach for you. I've been reading papers on ligament tears and dancers all night.'

Pippa's eyes filled with tears. 'Oh, Mum. I…'

Amelia gave her a hug. 'I know. This probably feels like the end of everything, but it's not. It's just a little bump in the road. Six months is nothing. This time next year, Principal Dancer Pippa Barnes will be getting rave reviews on the stage of the Fitzroy again. And you'll do the first two weeks of rehab with me—either I'll come and stay with you, or you can come back home for a couple of weeks, whichever you'd prefer.'

'But you can't! You've got work,' Pippa said.

'I've already organised a locum to cover me. You're more important,' Amelia said. 'And I'm not leaving you to struggle alone with crutches.'

She smiled. 'Besides, it'll be a lot easier for me to nag you to keep your foot raised above the level of your heart if we're actually in the same house.'

'I never expected...' Pippa shuddered. 'I mean, I know I disappointed you and Dad. The first in three generations of our family not to be a doctor.'

'Dancing,' Amelia said, 'is a very uncertain career. We only wanted the best for you. Yes, we had huge doubts. But I apologise, because I can see now we were wrong to hold you back. And, just so you know, you're not a disappointment. You're a very bright shining star, and I've always thought you're more than capable of doing absolutely anything you put your mind to.'

Pippa rubbed the tears from her eyes. 'Don't. I'm trying to be brave.'

'Of course you're brave. You get on stage six nights a week and bare your soul under the spotlight,' Amelia said. 'You're going to get through this. I've got your back. So have your sisters and your dad.'

And this time Pippa let the tears fall freely.

The surgery was successful, and Pippa went to stay with her parents. Her father shocked her even more than her mother had, by spending time playing cards with her and chatting, keeping her mind busy.

She missed dancing more than she could have believed possible.

And she missed Rory even more.

But she'd been the one to end it. And she'd taken his number off her phone so she wouldn't be tempted to call him.

The following week, Amelia checked a text message at the breakfast table. 'That television programme you were doing bits of—Holly says it's being screened tonight.'

Oh, no. Pippa didn't think she could bear to watch it.

But it seemed she didn't have a choice.

And it was all there. The history, the clips of famous ballet dancers, her teaching him to dance. Rory grumbling, 'Even when I'm cleaning my teeth, I hear your voice saying, "Straight knees!" or "Shoulders down!" and find myself checking my posture.' And the two of them dancing the 'Rose Adagio' on the Fitzroy's stage, the glorious music and their faces shining with love as they spun round the stage… She had to clench her fists to stop herself weeping.

'You really do have a special talent,' her father remarked.

The praise she'd so desperately longed for.

And it wasn't enough, any more. Nothing was enough, without Rory.

'And he's such a nice young man,' Amelia added. 'You must have enjoyed working with him.'

'I did.' And how she ached for him now. How she missed him. But she was doing the right thing for both of them, keeping her distance, she reminded herself. He wanted a family. She'd given him the freedom to find someone who'd give him what he needed.

She became aware that both her parents were looking at her expectantly.

'I'll have to send him—well, it can't be flowers. Not with his wasp allergy. Champagne,' she said.

Because it would only be polite to congratulate him on his series, wouldn't it?

'Delivery for me?' Rory was surprised, but accepted the box the runner brought in from reception. 'Thanks.'

He opened the box to find a card.

Congratulations on the series. Pippa.

Beneath the card was a moulded pulp bottle protector, and inside that was a bottle of champagne.

So she'd watched the show last night? He hadn't been able to watch it—seeing them dancing the 'Rose Adagio' together would've just been too hard, since she'd turned him down.

But if she'd watched it and she'd sent him champagne on same-day delivery, that had to mean something? You wouldn't go to that much trouble if it didn't really matter to you.

Did she miss him as much as he missed her? he wondered. Or was he just trying to convince himself that he hadn't got her completely wrong? Maybe he should just be sensible and keep his distance. At least that way he wouldn't get hurt again. He'd be foolish to jump to the conclusion that champagne meant she missed him. That it was some kind of coded message: fizzy, dizzy, just like their dance...

'Ooh, bubbles! Very nice,' Kenise said, walking into the office. 'Who are they from?'

'Pippa.'

'Uh-huh.' She raised her eyebrows. 'Are you going to call her?'

He shook his head. 'I'll text her.'

'I'm not going to pry,' Kenise said, 'but it's very obvious that something's happened between you. You've been miserable for days. I bet it's been the same for her.' She sighed. 'I like her and I think she's good for you. So whatever the row was about...'

Pippa had turned down his proposal of marriage. Flatly. Completely.

And he didn't want to talk about it.

Kenise shook her head. 'Sweetie, you can't sort out a fight by text, or even a phone call. Go and see her. Talk to her, face to face.'

He wasn't sure that Pippa would want to talk to him. He fell back on an excuse, even though it sounded utterly lame. It *was* utterly lame. 'I don't know where she is.'

Kenise scoffed. 'She's like you. If anything upsets her, I reckon she'll bury herself in work.'

Just as he did. He pushed the thought away that he and Pippa were two halves of the same whole. 'She can't. The ballet company's on their summer break, and the roof's being fixed.'

'The roof isn't going to affect the studio. And dancers are paranoid about keeping themselves dance-fit. You know exactly where she'll be,' Kenise said. 'Just go. I'll field anything that comes in.'

Was sending him champagne Pippa's way of reaching out to him? After all, she could've ignored the show completely. Or just sent him a congratulations card.

The more he thought about it, the more he wondered.

But the bottom line was that he *missed* her.

To hell with his pride. He'd take the risk and talk to her.

So he went to the Fitzroy.

Pippa wasn't there, but Nathalie Charrier was in her office. 'Pippa won't be here for weeks,' she said.

'Why?' Rory asked.

'Why did you want to see her?' Nathalie countered.

'She sent me champagne. I wanted to say thank you in person.'

'You'll have to text her instead,' Nathalie said, offhand.

Rory sighed. 'All right. Saying thank you in person was just a feeble excuse. I…miss her.'

Nathalie folded her arms. 'What did you do to upset her?'

'I'll tell you,' he bargained, 'if you tell me why she's not in the studio with everyone else.'

'Agreed,' Nathalie said. 'You first.'

He told her.

Her mouth thinned, and she told him what had happened at the end of Act Three.

Pippa had rescued him. Now it was his turn to rescue her from the devastation she must feel after her injury. 'I need to see her,' he said. 'Where is she?'

'I'd be breaking every Data Protection Act rule in the book if I told you,' Nathalie said, standing up and going to a filing cabinet. 'But perhaps,' she continued, fishing out a file and leaving it on her desk, 'the address of her next of kin might be a *petit* clue.' She muttered something Rory didn't quite catch, particularly as it was in French; knowing how acerbic Pippa's boss could be, he assumed it was something along the lines of '*petit*, just like your masculine brain'. It wasn't strictly fair; Pippa had been the one to call a halt. Then again, maybe he'd rushed her. Now he'd had time to think about it, hadn't she admitted to him that she didn't think she had space for both love and ballet in her life? Had he pushed her too fast, so she'd thought she had to choose?

If they talked it through, were completely honest with each other, he could show her that he was prepared to wait. To support her dreams. To compromise. And then maybe she'd be prepared to take a chance on him.

'Excuse me a moment,' Nathalie said. 'I'll just fetch a glass of water.'

Rory smiled, and the second she'd left her office he picked up the file. The one containing Pippa's personal details, including her next of kin.

He blinked as he read it. She was staying with her *parents*?

Well, OK.

He noted the address on his phone.

'You might also like to know,' Nathalie said, coming back into the office, 'that she's been promoted to Principal Dancer.'

He hadn't known that, either. 'Did that happen before or after her injury?' he asked, replacing the file on her desk and keeping his tone casual.

'I told her on the Wednesday morning.'

The day he'd proposed to her. She'd known about her promotion, but she hadn't told him she'd met her goals. Hurt flared, but he damped it down. This wasn't about him; it was about *her*.

'I also made her promise to keep it confidential because I'd announced it at the end of the Saturday show,' Nathalie said.

There were times when Pippa would play completely by the rules. An embargo was definitely one of them. So maybe she'd wanted to tell him, but felt she couldn't break her promise to her boss.

'Which I did,' Nathalie added with a sigh. '*After* I'd sent her to hospital.'

'Hang on.' Rory was shocked. 'Are you telling me she didn't even get to be there for her big moment?'

'I'll redo the announcement just before her next performance on my stage,' Nathalie said.

'However long it takes until then. I value her.' She folded her arms again and fixed him with a stare. 'Hurt her, and you'll be dealing with me.'

'I won't,' Rory said, 'I'll keep you posted. And thank you.'

'Don't let me down,' Nathalie said. 'Make her shine again.'

Rory wasn't taking any chances. He'd also noted Amelia Barnes' mobile phone number. He texted her to introduce himself—on the grounds that most people wouldn't answer a number they didn't recognise, but might read a text—and asked her to call him. Five minutes later his phone shrilled.

It was an illuminating conversation, on both sides.

He went home via the florist's, picked up his car and drove to Pippa's parents' house. Amelia answered the doorbell.

'You've got ten minutes,' she said. 'But if you hurt—'

'I'm not going to,' he interrupted gently. 'And besides, you'd have to fight for your place in the queue. I'm not sure of your chances against Nathalie Charrier—or my own mother, come to that, despite the fact that she hasn't met Pippa yet.'

To his surprise, Amelia grinned—and he could really see where Pippa got her smile.

'You'll do,' she said. 'She's in the living room. First door on the right. I'll be in the kitchen if you need anything.' She looked pointedly at his feet.

'Shoes off,' he said. 'Got it.'

Pippa looked up as the door opened. 'Mum—oh!' she said, shocked to see Rory.

'Wait—I need to do this properly,' he said, and did a couple of the turns she'd taught him for the 'Rose Adagio' routine before presenting her the bouquet with a flourish.

'Oh, Rory,' she said, her voice catching.

'Don't cry,' he warned, 'because Nathalie is terrifying, your mum's roughly on the same level, and so is mine. If there's a single teardrop from you, between the three of them, I'll be in fear of my life.'

'Don't be ridiculous,' she said, but she couldn't help smiling.

'I didn't know about your ankle until a couple of hours ago,' he said. 'I'm sorry. That's hard.'

'It's character-forming,' she said. 'And in a way it kind of did me a favour. Because now I know I'm not a—' her voice wobbled '—disappointment to my family.'

'I could've told you that, even though I haven't met them. Well, I had a short but very useful conversation with your mother, when I left Nathalie,' he said. 'By the way, congratulations on making Principal Dancer.'

'Nathalie told you that, too?'

He nodded. 'She said she'd given you the news unofficially on Wednesday.'

So he knew she'd kept it from him. 'I wanted to tell you, but Nathalie swore me and Yuki to secrecy,' she said.

'She told me,' he said. 'I've been thinking. Being Principal Dancer means you're going to be travelling a bit more, at least for a few years. With a decent internet connection, any writing or researching I happen to do can take place anywhere. And it's up to me to arrange interviews. They might just turn out to be with people who live somewhere near wherever you're performing on tour.'

Was he telling her that he'd fit his career around hers? 'What are you saying?' she asked carefully.

'I'm saying that my feelings for you haven't changed. I love you, Pippa Barnes. It's nothing to do with the fact that you saved my life—it's you. The brightness in you that makes everything around you sparkle. I want *you*.'

She lifted her chin, knowing they needed to confront the big issues. 'But you want a family.'

'And you don't?'

That was the thing. 'I hadn't even thought

about it before I met you. I was focused on becoming Principal Dancer.' And she'd got there.

'And now?'

'I want a family. *But...*' And this was the important thing. 'I'm not ready yet. Maybe I won't be ready for a couple of years—and by that I mean a couple of years after I can dance again. It might be six months from now until I've healed well enough to do that.' She dragged in a breath. 'I don't want to disappoint you, Rory, the way I've disappointed my family.'

'The thing is—and you've told me you know this now,' he said, 'your family *weren't* actually disappointed in you. They're just not very good at articulating their feelings.'

That stung. 'And you are?'

'I make my living from words. I'm articulate. I can use words of one beat, if you want me to,' he said, and grinned. 'Or we can have polysyllabic conversations, if that's your preference.'

'OK. You've made your point,' she said.

'Yes, I want children,' he said. 'With you. But I'm happy to wait until you're ready. And I'd also like you to know that I don't expect you to give up your career for me. You've put in years of hard work to get where you are, and I understand that—I've done the same. So we'll work it out together. We might need a bit of help to run the house, and maybe a nanny and a personal assistant—but we'll be a team and we can make it work the way we want it to.'

She was silent, thinking about it. A team. Making it work, together.

'You turned me down when I asked you to marry me,' he said. 'And maybe I rushed you, because when I realised what I felt about you I wanted everything, right then, all at once. But I can be patient. Because I love you,' he said. 'I want to be with you. Life without you is like trudging through murky slush, the day after it snows. And I'm prepared to wait until you're ready—because you're worth it.'

'You love me,' she said, almost in wonder. She'd pushed him away, and he still loved her.

'And you're killing me here,' he said. 'Was I wrong about our 'Rose Adagio'?'

'No. You weren't,' she said. 'It worked because I'd fallen in love with you, and it showed.'

'So you do actually love me back?'

'Yes,' she said. Knowing that words were important to him, she added, 'I love you, too.'

'And the only reason you turned me down is because you're not ready to have children, and you didn't think I wanted to wait? When you could have talked to me about it, and I would've told you that I would?' he checked.

She squirmed. 'Yes. And I've learned from

that: next time I make an assumption, I'll talk to you.'

'Good,' he said. 'I think we're on the road to being safe from Nathalie and our mums combined. Almost, but not quite.' He paused. 'Pippa Barnes, I know we've only known each other for a couple of months, but it's enough for me to be sure of what I want. I love you. Will you marry me?'

And this time, she smiled and said, 'Yes.'

EPILOGUE

Five years later

RORY SAT IN the auditorium of the Fitzroy Theatre, his toddler daughter Aurora on his lap, while the dress rehearsal of *Sleeping Beauty* unfolded on the stage in front of them. It was the traditional version, where the 'Rose Adagio' was danced with her four suitors. Though he would always love the version he'd danced with Pippa on this stage.

'Mummy dance,' Aurora informed him solemnly.

'Yes.'

'Mummy princess.'

'Yes,' he agreed. 'She's dancing as someone called Princess Aurora.'

Aurora frowned. '*Me* Rora.'

He nodded. 'You were named after her. She's our favourite princess.'

'Rora dance with Mummy?' Aurora asked.

'Later,' he promised.

She looked pleased. 'Daddy dance baby swans too?'

He chuckled. Practically as soon as Aurora could walk unaided, she'd started to dance—and she loved it when the three of them did the 'Dance of the Little Swans' together.

'We'll do the baby swans,' he said. 'When we get home.'

Aurora clapped, then settled back on his lap to watch her mother dance across the stage.

And life, Rory thought, couldn't get any more perfect.

* * * * *

*If you enjoyed this story,
check out these other great reads
from Kate Hardy*

A Fake Bride's Guide to Forever
Wedding Deal with Her Rival
Tempted by Her Fake Fiancé
Crowning His Secret Princess

All available now!

Harlequin® Reader Service

Enjoyed your book?

Try the perfect subscription for Romance readers and get more great books like this delivered right to your door.

See why over 10+ million readers have tried Harlequin Reader Service.

Start with a Free Welcome Collection with free books and a gift—valued over $20.

Choose any series in print or ebook. See website for details and order today:

TryReaderService.com/subscriptions